Also by Shelby Hearon

Armadillo in the Grass
The Second Dune
Hannah's House
Now and Another Time
A Prince of a Fellow
Painted Dresses
Afternoon of a Faun
Group Therapy
A Small Town
Five Hundred Scorpions
Owning Jolene
Hug Dancing
Life Estates
Footprints

Ella in Bloom

Ella in Bloom

Shelby Hearon

Alfred A. Knopf   NewYork 2001

Portions of the novel appeared as "Uncle Karl" in the Southwest Review.

Library of Congress Cataloging-in-Publication Data
Hearon, Shelby.
Ella in bloom / by Shelby Hearon — 1st ed.
p.   cm.
ISBN 0-375-41038-4
1. Mothers and daughters—Louisiana—Fiction.   2. Single mothers—Fiction.
3. Louisiana—Fiction.   4. Texas—Fiction.   I. Title.
PS3558.E256 E45 2000
813'.54—dc21   00-020311

Manufactured in the United States of America
First Edition

To my husband,
William Halpern,
with my love

*I am grateful for the
Writer's Voice Residency Award
that helped to support this work.*

The real interest of the myths is that they lead us back to a time when the world was young and people had a connection with the earth, with trees and seas and flowers and hills, unlike anything we ourselves can feel. When the stories were being shaped, we are given to understand, little distinction had as yet been made between the real and the unreal.

—EDITH HAMILTON, *Mythology*

Ella in Bloom

❧ Old Metairie

1

I made a rose garden for my mother.

Redolent old roses blooming against a weathered low brick wall. (Perhaps I'd say the bricks were from a once-fine country home, now crumbling against crape myrtle, or perhaps I'd say from some eighteenth-century church, fallen into disuse in an unsavory area in the heart of the parish.) Such care I took throughout that spring and early summer, steeping myself in the history of Chinas, Teas, Albas, Gallicas, Bourbons, Noisettes. Reading about botanists who brought back cuttings from China, prizewinning rosarians who could trace the ancestry of their present best rose back to the *jardins* of the Empress Josephine. I learned to decipher the tiny notations in the antique-rose catalogues I kept by my bed, signifying scent, hue, hips, *remontancy*—a lovely, lingering word meaning to flower again, meaning possessed of a second chance to bloom.

Sometimes, immersed in my invention, my hands would

move as if handling real flowers, and I would arrange in the air bouquets of the old roses, clustering near-chocolate mauves, ecrus like faded parchment, dusty pinks, creamy whites, until I could almost see them. Until I sometimes actually walked out my back screened door into the oppressive, steamy coastal Louisiana heat, expecting to find that brick wall, the dark thick foliage, those abundant fragrant flowers.

All this was background, of course, me soaking myself in the subject until I had the right small details (casual as a pencil sketch on a paper napkin) to set the scene. The scene I hoped my mother imagined me, Ella, her younger and now only daughter, to inhabit. Me, once dismissed as difficult (mule-headed), wayward, willful, now, by default, back in her contingent, if not entirely good, graces, composing a conciliatory letter home.

Often, I would make mention of some favorite linen skirt or dress. *Linen,* as evocative a word as *roses.* Whereas, in fact, the last actual linen garment I'd worn had been the black button-front dress I'd stolen for my sister Terrell's memorial service. Even at the time (stunned almost to bruising by the unexpected loss), I was unable, looking at the appalling catchall contents of my own closet, to bear the thought of my mother saying: "How could you show up looking like that, at your own sister's funeral?"

My actual life here in Old Metairie didn't get a mention. If I hadn't ended up destitute, as my parents predicted when I ran away to get married ("throwing your life away on a worthless boy who is never going to amount"), still, the house I occupied half of on the scruffy, run-down, not yet

gentrified fringes of a safe, secluded *resaca* of a neighborhood was not something to write home about. Considering
that it sat on an unpaved service road which ran along a railroad track and a bayou and dead-ended on the only through
street in the area, one that allowed access by vagrants,
thieves, and the rest of the working world. The reason I
stayed put and paid the killing property taxes? So that my
daughter, Birdie, could attend the local school, fairly good
and uncrowded, since most of the local children, naturally,
were sent to private schools.

At the moment, pen in hand, I was sitting in the kitchen
at the back of the house, mouthing *Dear Mother, Dear Mother,*
and looking out at my actual yard, a scrap of high grass partially shaded by the branches of a neighbor's sagging willow
and by our own overgrown oleander (whose leaves were
purported to be poisonous to children and animals). There
was a little pea-gravel square that must once have been the
start of a patio, and now was at least a place where, in cool,
less steamy weather, my daughter and a friend could get
away from me, or I could sit with this realtor guy who
sometimes came around. I recalled reading some book in
which the old woman (a char lady?) stayed in the unheated
house all day long, only lighting the grate fire in the evening
when her husband was due. They found her cold in her cold
house. I was not really sweltering here in my shorts and
T-shirt with no bra, my oak-brown hair pulled up on my
head with a bandana, waiting until my daughter came home
from her class to turn on the frigid, clammy window AC
unit. It was just that the sound of the motor running seemed
to me the sound of dollars disappearing. Most days when I

was home, I made do with the ceiling fan and a glass of iced coffee. Besides, it hardly did to complain about the stultifying Gulf Coast humidity (the way sweat stood on your arms and legs as if you'd come from a shower, the way you breathed damp air as if in a steam bath), knowing that Texas had been in the grip of a dreadful, unrelenting, baking drought for a hundred days already. Hard for me, gone so long, to imagine: I always saw my mother in her own cultivated garden, ablaze with pink and red azaleas.

Buddy, my sometime husband, got it in his mind that my folks thought he was no good because he got me to run off, but the truth more likely was that I ran off with him because my folks thought he was no good. At any rate, I owed him forever for getting me out of their house, away from Texas, on my own two feet. He'd made what living he made repossessing yachts for a repo outfit that operated out of Florida. Sometimes he got a windfall; sometimes he lost our shirts. I did nothing, which is what I knew how to do, and waited for him to show up again, to fall into bed with me again. One day a woman whose yacht he'd snatched asked him did he know someone could water her houseplants while she got out of town for a spell. He told her that was my specialty. "She's trained in horticulture," he said. At that time the only plant I'd ever watered had been a runty ruby begonia I'd drowned. From such beginnings came careers.

His bad end had some upside. The last time he left me, he left me pregnant, for which I still gave daily thanks. And, since he never bothered to dissolve our legal entanglement, he also left me with an insurance policy that let me buy this elderly duplex and get my Chevy overhauled. News of his death out in the Gulf aboard someone's delinquent sailboat came to me not by way of his mother, who might have forgotten my name, but from the woman he'd been living with, who thought he might have gone back home. The whole thing was sad, including what felt like everyone's relief. My daughter Birdie could say that her daddy was dead, instead of that she never saw him and didn't know him from Adam. And my mother could discreetly recast me as a "young widow from Louisiana," or so my sister had reported. Mostly I hated his being gone because even now I would probably be holding a crumb of hope that one day he, Buddy Marshall, might blow back in along with the summer's first hurricane and decide he'd like to stick around and get to know his family.

Earlier today, my mind a blank, I'd gone to find a new rose to tell Mother about. Old Metairie, steamy and sunken and surrounded by waters (the Mississippi, Lake Pontchartrain, the squalling Gulf), was infatuated with old roses. I could have asked most anyone. Some of the homes where I plant-tended had rose arbors and shrubs on their grounds, past reflecting pools and pebbled paths. But I would never have asked one of the women who hired me; I was just another of the several helpers who came in when they fled the stifling summer heat, taking off for the mountains, to Europe, to the rocky coast of Maine: house sitter, pet sitter, plant sitter, security service. My favorite source was Henry (Henri), the head rose gardener at Belle Vue, a stately mansion with a series of lavish old gardens through which strolled peacocks and in the branches of whose trees songbirds made their nests. For a nominal fee, the grounds were open to the public, including me. He always had something for me, and, in return, I offered a pair of ears into which he could pour the story of his family's centuries in France, the likelihood that a great-great-grandfather had been gardener to the Empress Josephine.

Today he'd told me how the rose fanciers were bringing him their summer finds, something they spotted up a dirt road outside Shreveport, something growing on the wooden side of an AME church in Tuscaloosa. "Everybody thinks they have an Old Blush," he said, shaking his sunbaked face to indicate they usually didn't. I told him I was looking for something new. "Just got this in from England." He showed me a nearly perfect quartered rose, deep pink to fading palest pink. It didn't smell like tea (like the Teas) or banana (like the Chinas); it smelled—well, like a rose. "It came out of Hamburg when that was part of Denmark, an Alba bred with a Damask, likely. The Brits call it Queen of Denmark. I don't know what the Danes call it." We laughed. Queen of England? He touched the blue-green leaves. "Flourishes anywhere."

The very first time I stopped to talk to Henry, and to watch him prune, clip, pinch faded blooms, he showed me one of his prizes, the Natchitoches Noisette, which had been grown from a clipping found near an old fort that went back to the 1700s. Its cupped pink flowers smelled, he said, of myrrh. I was enchanted: who had an inkling of the odor of myrrh? I went straight home and wrote of the rose to my mother—and that was the beginning of my correspondence garden.

Did she visualize rosebushes against a wall? Did she

repeat their names? Did the thought of them take her back to her girlhood in East Texas, not unlike our part of Louisiana? Or did I only hope that at the least she was not sorry to receive my letters?

In January, in a blustery wind the week after the funeral, I'd bought a box of heavy notepaper at the Belle Vue gift shop. Soon, I would need another. Getting out a sheet, I saw that my hands were so damp I'd be bound to smudge the ink. I wiped them, and then, giving in, turned the window unit to high to dry myself, cool myself, enough to write. First lifting my arms over my head to dry the undersides, then leaning over to get the back of my neck. I held a cube of ice to my cheek. *Dear Mother, Dear Mother.* The sweating wasn't only from the heat. Part of it was from the effort of dissembling, at the age of forty-three, as if I were a child of ten lying about her friends, her grades, what her teacher said.

Dear Mother,

I worry about you and Daddy in the dreadful heat. I hope you are managing. And what of your poor yard?

My roses all flourish in our heat (even if we don't) because they get plenty of moisture and the nights are cool. I have added a new rose, over against the west wall, where there was a break in the bricks and where the soil seemed a little thin, an English hybrid called Queen of Denmark. Silk-soft, pale pink, it perfumes the air wherever planted.

Did I mention to you I got a spot on my favorite linen dress? An ivory Moygashel with a square neck and gored skirt. I used a bit of soap and cold water, and hope to be able to wear it to White Linen Night. This is a fundraising event for all the Old Metairie garden clubs, and a very nice social evening to which a young widow like myself can feel comfortable going alone.

Birdie—as I believe I told you Robin is calling herself—is taking cello lessons this summer. Such a good thing, for a girl to have a musical proficiency.

Please take care of yourself and Daddy.

Love,

Ella

ONE VIOLET LANE
OLD METAIRIE

2

I was on my way to take a shower when the phone rang. "Hello," I said, trying to sound upbeat. Every call was a potential job.

"Guten Tag."

Daddy. My daddy. "Hi," I answered, trying not to choke on the word. This was an old routine. Daddy and Mother, on some trip abroad, had found a card in a hotel room translating *Good Morning* into French, German, and English: *Bonjour, Guten Tag, Hi*. They'd thought that a good joke and shared it with my sister and me. A half century it seemed ago, when the world was young. I wiped my eyes with the back of my hand.

Maybe he was doing the same. Families weren't supposed to divorce one another.

"Your mother——," he began, then coughed a bit, cleared his throat.

"——How is Mother doing?" I blew my nose.

"She wants you to come for her birthday. You and——" He coughed again.

"Birdie," I reminded him, the new name my daughter had adopted. What her daddy had called her, when he had. I'd mentioned it in January, but how could it have registered at such a time? Robin, her given name, was what my sister had longed to be called—a movie-star name, she'd said, a fashion-model name. She'd never liked hers, Terrell. In school her teachers had thought it a boy's name or called her Terry. Her married name, Terrell Hall, she claimed, sounded like a freshman dorm. I'd given her my daughter's name as a gift, but by then it hadn't mattered.

"She has it in her mind, your mother, to have all her grandchildren together for the occasion. It's been a spell, a long spell it seems to me, since we had a proper celebration."

"Daddy," I protested, "that's only two weeks away. I can't leave my watering jobs. And trying to get a ticket this late—"

The trip back for the funeral had been a nightmare: the absence of Terrell everywhere. Mother barely speaking, Daddy broken-down weeping, my sister's husband and her big boys walking stiff and stunned in their dark suits. Sleeping again in the double room I'd once shared upstairs had been claustrophobic. Passing out coffee after the service, the trivial had blurred with the tragic: I musn't spill anything on the black button-front dress I'd pilfered; my sister would never be back.

"I wouldn't want you to pay for the tickets," my daddy said. "You can't have an easy time of it, a woman on her own." He sounded genuinely worried, as if he'd just learned I'd been thrown out on the street.

"Really, I couldn't—" I tried to think. For the funeral, I'd driven most of the night to get there; Birdie and I had slept in the car and cleaned up at a hickory-smoked-hamburger stand on the outskirts of Austin. I couldn't do that again. But even with free tickets, it cost money to travel. July and August were my busiest times of the year; I couldn't cancel a job. And what would I wear? Where were the linen dresses of my letters?

Where indeed.

"That's my present to your mother. Getting all the young ones here." Daddy cleared his throat again. I could imagine him, stooped, as very tall men became, thinning white hair and beard, probably wearing a dress shirt and vest even in the house, professor's clothes, to make the call. "You had a good visit with your sister last year at this time, of which we got a full report. But your mother and I are behind in our catching up. When you were here for the—for her—" His voice caught.

"We'll come," I told him. "Of course."

Off the phone, in the muggy, chilly, air-cooled kitchen, I made myself a glass of iced coffee, the leftover breakfast brew. I looked in my closet and quickly shut the door. I decided to wash my hair in the shower and then comb it out, see how bad the ends were and how shapeless the mane. "Can't you do something with that hair, dear?" had been a refrain of my mother's all the time I lived at home. Maybe Buddy taking it in his hands, burying his face in it, saying, "Don't ever cut this stuff, hear me, you've got million-dollar hair," was all it took for me to pack my bag and run away.

However, Daddy's invitation raised a problem more serious than either my strapped finances or my frazzled appearance: the matter of my sister Terrell's purported visit to see me last summer in Old Metairie. She had called me, at first I thought just to say hello, about a year ago, shortly after the Fourth, to say she was telling them all—Mom and Dad and Rufus, her husband—that she was coming to see me, that she meant to get back in touch with her baby sister Ella. But that she wasn't really making a trip to see me. That she had a man. "You musn't think bad things about me. We're head over heels in love and I never ever had that before, the way you did with Buddy. He makes me feel so young; I'm out of my mind." They had been trying to get together for just about absolutely *forever*, she said, and now at last they'd arranged this weekend to New Orleans. Did I think she was just awful?

"Who is he?" I'd asked, not wanting a name, just wanting some clue, I guess, of how come she'd picked him. It made me nervous, and more than a little bit sad, to hear about her doing this. I still thought of her husband, back when he was just a law student called Red, as the one friend I'd had before I left home. He used to confide to me how crazy about Terrell he was and I used to confess to him how bad I wanted to get out of there, that house and family that he was wanting so much to marry into.

"I won't tell you his name, Ella. Then you can't let anything slip. But I can tell you this much, he comes from the very same county Daddy does, Ector County, from a little town called *Notrees*. I'm not kidding. I guess that's what got me first, that West Texas twang. He says where he grew up is a sort of desert with old meteor craters and no oil. Though everybody out there has to tell you they haven't got producing wells on their place. He and his daddy grow beef and now they're farming emus, which are just like overgrown chickens, he says. He says they raise them for leather, but then they have to use the leather for gloves and chaps to keep the birds from ripping an arm or leg off with those toenails.

"We met on a sailing weekend, and right away as soon as I saw him, I just about went out of my mind over him. I wasn't looking or anything, but, between us, privately, things haven't been all that great at home. Now that Rufus has quit the law firm, he's sort of gone crazy on me. You don't know how that is, because, well, Buddy wasn't, you know, in the mainstream to begin with. But when middle-aged men change their spots, if you get what I mean, it's like they just turn into somebody else overnight. We hardly have one word to say anymore, and the boys don't know what's going on. So, anyway, it's taken me and Mr. Emu, I'll call him, nearly *forever* to get together, but we've finally got it all planned. You have to promise me you'll never *ever* tell, no matter what—"

I'd done my best to stay in touch with Terrell over the years. After all, your sisters or brothers, whoever you had, were the people who went down the same road with you all the way. You came into your parents' lives after things had already happened; the people they'd once been were gone and the people they were you couldn't really know. And it must be the same with your children. You were already set when they showed up, you were opaque to them, they were in another time zone from you. But siblings, they were on the same boat, in the same car, skating down the same side-walk from the start.

"Cross my heart," I said. Not really warm about my role in this—I wasn't into lying about someone else's life on top of my own. But I asked, "What do you want me to do?" Trying to figure out if I was going to get to see her at all. It had been four years then since I'd last been home.

"You'll have to send me a picture of your place, you know, and tell me something about the house I can pass on to Mom, who'll want to hear everything. And make up some stuff we went to see, so I can tell her and Dad, and Rufus and the boys. And maybe something about Robin?"

"She's calling herself Birdie now," I mentioned. "She's learning to play the cello." That being the one true thing I always told. "Look," I said, "why don't I meet you at the airport? I could bring photos of my place and Birdie, and we could get someone to take a shot of us together?" I hesitated, then said it straight out, "Hey, I'd like to see you."

Terrell said she just couldn't. "We've only got two nights. We're flying in together and we'll be lucky if we can wait till we get to the hotel."

"Sure, okay." I understood. Still, I was disappointed. "It's just—been a long time, Ter."

"I know, I'm sorry. Honestly. I get so busy and it seems like we have people from West Texas and the Hill Country coming to the lake every weekend to sail. Just to see *water*. You have no idea what this drought has been like."

At first I thought maybe she didn't want me to see this guy from Notrees. That she might be keeping him from me, since I was more available, being single. You get this between sisters, sometimes, worry about the competition. Buddy had actually first started hanging around the house trying to get a date with her, before he and I got a lot of chemistry going, a lot of heat. Luckily, she didn't go for the futureless type. And Red and I, her present husband Rufus and I, used to go out for hamburgers when she wasn't home and talk about was she ever going to marry him or not, and talk about how could I leave home without finishing school or knowing how to do anything.

But after I got off the phone, I'd realized that the fact was she didn't want *him,* this Mr. Emu, to see *me.* Didn't want to be embarrassed by her tatty younger sister. If she'd gone up a notch in her marriage from where we came from (the history professor daddy and the gardening mother), then I'd gone down a notch or two in my scrambling solo life. I could see that one of the advantages of a secret lover was that he didn't have to meet your kin.

So I did exactly what she asked for. In the same manner that I now wrote letters to my mother, practically coming to believe them myself, so I carefully built up all the details of a wonderful weekend reunion with my sister Terrell. I sent her photos to show around of "my" pink-painted cottage on one of Old Metairie's nicest magnolia-shaded streets, the sort of house—with white picket fence, white shutters on the floor-to-ceiling windows, pots of waxy white Cape jasmine by the door—to which my mother could point with pride. The sort of home, classy but not large, dear but not overpriced, in which a sociable young widow might live a pleasant life in the Deep South. I wrote describing a late supper in a French restaurant called the Pink Cafe, where I had never eaten; early communion at the old Episcopal church, because Mother loved old churches, modeled stone by stone after St. Bartolph's in Cambridge, England, that I often drove by; and a benefit high tea in the rose gardens at historic Belle Vue, whose grounds I did know well.

I constructed that weekend never dreaming that I would be called upon to repeat the story again and again at my sister's funeral. That I would have to recount to everyone where we went, what we saw, our breakfasts of fresh strawberries and cream on my pink patio, looking out at my walled summer garden.

Telling all this to her husband had been the very worst. My parents were too stunned, too staggered by their grief, to be able to listen for long. My mother had to hold herself together, straight and composed, for her daughter's friends; my daddy had to make coffee and apple kuchen for the remnants of family. But my old friend Red was someone I had never lied to, was the one person in my past I could always come to with the whole (unsavory, shocking, or ordinary) truth. And he was the one who seemed to hang on my words. No longer the law student I remembered, with horn-rim glasses, shaggy dark hair, white shirts with the sleeves rolled up above his elbows, corduroy pants, usually with a casebook under his arm, as if to prove he was what he claimed to be. He still sat, intent, the way he used to, leaning forward, his forearms on his knees, but now in a well-tailored black suit, good shoes, an expensive haircut, discreet contact lenses. His once-tanned face had been blanched with shock and his once-voluble conversation muted, but, still, after his subdued greeting, "Hello, Ella," he'd stayed close, listening while I retold the tale of the weekend reunion in Old Metairie. Hearing my daddy lean down and say, "I'm glad you daughters had a get-together." His eyes wet. Hearing my mother, wearing winter white, the mourning of another era, say to a friend, her voice shaking slightly, "The girls had such a nice visit, only last summer."

And all the time wondering what my sister had told them. And wondering, too, if anyone else knew who she'd been going to see that bitter January when her little chartered Piper Cherokee went down in the sleet.

3

Birdie had let herself in with the key she wore around her neck on a ribbon, and was in the kitchen by the time I had emerged from the shower and changed into my watering shorts and a clean T-shirt.

"Do you want a peanut butter sandwich, Mom?" My daughter did our lunches at home on the weekend; I did our suppers.

"Thank you," I said. "With banana."

She added bean sprouts to her sandwich, making them today on seven-grain bread, which tasted to me like brown paper sack.

"We're going to Austin for your grandmother's birthday," I told her, knowing that if we missed a Saturday, she missed a Junior String Project class.

"Why are we going to do that? Last time we went to see Grandmom, you cried all the way home."

"It was my sister's funeral."

"I think," she suggested, "you cried because you don't get on with your mom."

"That, too."

"So how come we're going to go?"

"My daddy called." *Guten Tag.* "He's sending us tickets."

"Is that nice, to let Granddaddy do that?"

What was *nice?* The major existential question. And something I'd been reprimanded for not being by both my mother and my daughter, birds of such different feathers.

"He wants us to be there," I said.

"Okay," she decided, eating the seven-grain crusts I'd left on my plate.

"I need a dress." I stared down at my watering shorts.

Birdie cleared our plates and helped herself to orange juice. "Felice's mom, who sews? She says people take their old clothes to that resale shop in the Pink Mall. She sometimes makes things over, for Felice—?" She made a furrow between her eyes in her earnest desire to help.

It was a myth that people created their own children, the ball-of-clay business. The truth was, children made themselves in reaction to you. They detected the moth hole in your personality, the weak seam in your resolve, and they moved right in to make out of the whole cloth of their observation a better self than the one you had ready for them. I often found myself thinking, Can this be my child? This short, plump, bossy person with crinkled masses of light hair down to her waist, in an Amish-style dress dangling the length of her unshaved legs. A serious musician at fourteen.

A full-time problem solver.

"I could look into that," I agreed, thinking that a thrift shop made a lot of sense. Kissing her cheek, grabbing my car keys, I headed out the back door of the duplex into the sticky midday heat.

With some effort, I tried to loosen my shoulders and

check my watering notes. If I lately had increased anxiety about going into other people's homes and being, for the short period of time that I tended their houseplants, solely responsible for anything that happened (any damage to property, any breach in security), I had only myself to blame. But at least I no longer, as I once had, grew faint with fear that I'd never understand the plants placed in my care. Did they droop from thirst or soggy roots? Did they grow sideways searching for more light or seeking shade? What of a yellow leaf? Now I read them as easily as I did birds picking at fallen figs or cats sunning themselves on a stoop. Now with confidence I checked the leaves and blooms, loosened and tested the soil, gauged the light, let the tap water sit the fifteen minutes it took the chlorine to settle out.

My first home today was a stark modern (strange to see on Old Metairie's tree-lined streets) whose owners, from sun-dried California, were summering in the Alps. There I struggled to tend great specimen palms in heavy stone pots—*Kentias,* Chestnut *Dioöns,* King *Segos,* Ming *Aralias.* Difficult to heft around or shift to catch the natural daylight without throwing out my back. The second home, four blocks away, near the Old Metairie Country Club, was, in contrast, a pleasure. The interior courtyard fragrant with dwarf orange and lemon trees, Asian Japonica camellias, Persian white jasmine. The decorative fountain splashing the night-blooming moonflowers with their great dozing luminous blooms and the pale funnels of the Mandevilla.

At the third house, the scene of my crime, I punched in the code (the last four digits of my phone number) that had been programmed for me and carefully set inside six large cobalt-blue water jugs. As with any below-sea-level area (we were the lowlands of America), everyone had filtration and purification systems, reverse osmosis units, and, those who could afford it, purified drinking water delivered to the back door, much as milk had once been.

This house, which belonged to Mrs. Thibaud, my very first customer, was the place I had learned to love roses. She didn't have the old antique roses that Henry, the head gardener at Belle Vue, had, heirlooms with breeding lines going back through the centuries to a French empress, a Chinese emperor. But almost painfully lovely English hybrids nonetheless, as delicately colored as home-dyed Easter eggs.

I had been working here, at this imposing Georgian colonial, while the owners skied Vail, the day I'd heard about my sister's crash. And I just lost it. There I was, standing surrounded, suffocating from the incense of those papery pastel blooms, tears running down my face. Nothing was mine. Not the grand house, not the husband shepherding his grain facilities in St. Charles, St. James, and St. John the Baptist Parishes, not the matched pair of rare Chartreux cats who slept upstairs in a cool room far away from strangers, not even one single scented, cupped, and cabbagey rose. I didn't have any of this and a sudden feeling of overwhelming deprivation washed over me. A stand-in for the irreversible loss: I had no sister.

I felt I had to take something. Had to walk out that door with something that wasn't mine. Perhaps waifs who stole lipsticks in the mall had that same feeling: I deserve *something*. Setting down my watering can, my moisture gauge, I climbed the wide, curved stairway to the off-limits second floor. And in her closet (nice Mrs. Thibaud's walk-in closet), from a cluster of half a dozen black linen dresses, I took one. Folding it with care over my arm, I left the house. The roses would survive; they were more hardy than we.

I became obsessed with making sure my mother could not find fault with anything. With Birdie's help, I subdued my unruly nut-brown hair into a pinned-up French braid. I scraped together the money for a real manicure to undo the dirt damage to my knuckles and nails (remembering that Scarlett O'Hara got into trouble, despite making her green velvet drapes into a fancy dress, because her turnip-rooting hands were a giveaway).

After the service, back at my parents' house, I'd heard my mother say, a drenched lace-edged handkerchief dabbing her eyes, "Oh, and this is our other daughter, Ella," and she was not ashamed. To each of my mother's sympathetic friends, I held out a smooth hand. To each of my daddy's distressed colleagues, I offered my blushed and powdered cheek. The only time I broke down was when my mother peered at Birdie, a plump fourteen-year-old she'd last seen at age nine, and murmured, "My, hasn't she *grown*—"

When I returned the dress, unspotted, four days later, tucking it back between the sleeveless black shift and the black shawl-collared shirtwaist where I had left the empty padded hanger, I thought I must have been mad. My heart could not have beat faster if I'd opened the closet door and found half a dozen security guards waiting with drawn guns.

Even now, as I gave myself over to the pleasure of the rose-filled atrium, I took care to remember that nothing I handled was mine.

4

My friend the realtor, Karl Krauss, showed up at the back door in his shirtsleeves, saying he had a house he wanted me to see. He wasn't exactly a boyfriend, although he'd been a friend since he'd found the current tenant for my duplex, and although we provided occasional warmth of an intimate nature for one another. Trying to raise a daddy-less girl, I'd have welcomed almost any grown man of decent intent and sound mind, and for his part, heading for fifty with no dependents, the idea of being a surrogate uncle to Birdie had a big appeal.

Besides, I liked going around to houses with him; he enjoyed ferreting out the history of a place, seeing if it had been down-at-the-heels once and was now on its way back, or the other way around. He liked looking up the deed records; he liked hazarding a guess as to why neighborhoods changed. This information came in handy in selling—he could point out the home's fine past or its pricey future— but mostly he just got a kick out of digging around. It made his life, he said, something more than the detritus of a salesman.

"You want to come along with us, Bird?" he asked her.

"No thank you. Felice and I are going to the Pink Mall."

I couldn't object to my daughter and her friend hanging out at the small nearby square of specialty shops—stationery, gifts, candles, linens, socks—and eating places. They had older friends who worked as clerks or waiters, and they counted the days till they could do the same. Child labor laws did not take into account grown-up fourteen-year-olds who wanted to buy a cello or (Felice) flute of their own, good instruments, not String Project rebuilt loaners. My daughter made a little money baby-sitting, and, in the summer months, got paid to feed the cats of people escaping the steam-bath heat. Baby-sitting, cat-sitting, plant-sitting: we were a cottage industry.

"We don't have to hurry," Karl said, noticing that we were suddenly alone. "Nice and cool in here." He edged over and slipped an arm around my waist.

I shook my head. "The girls could show up." I was still undone by Daddy's call, by the idea of a trip back home. I didn't want to take off my clothes and make sex in the afternoon, just because we had the opportunity. I shut off the AC unit and grabbed my keys.

"I should have a place," he said, looking mournful. He'd been in the garage apartment behind his folks' house since a non-amicable divorce.

"Thanks for the thought," I told him.

I felt comfortable with Karl, that's probably why we'd lasted so long, in a casual way. True, he had that generally slick look of most realtors: barbershop haircut, rep tie, starched shirt, a jacket he could drape over a shoulder if needed; but behind that front, he appeared real enough.

He'd not had an easy life, and still had an ailing mother, a depressed dad at home, and a complaining ex. But he didn't paint the picture any darker than it was, and he could be cheered up by almost any kind of film. When Terrell died, he had provided me a lot of shoulder and not much talk. Both most welcome.

Plus he asked Birdie questions. A gift money couldn't buy.

"Why 'Birdie'?" he inquired, when she chose her new name.

"That's what my dad called me. Didn't he, Mom?"

"He did," I said. Truthful to an extent, recalling Buddy's former calls: How's the birdie these days? She look like you? You living with anybody? This had been something she seemed to need in recent years, stories about her daddy.

"I have a friend called Oisie who says that's Birdie in French," she told him. She pronounced it "wee-see" and flapped her hands.

"The head cheerleader in my high school was named Robin. She was something special."

"You ever have a date with her?"

"Would I be here if I had?"

"You might be, Karl. You don't know that you wouldn't be." A foot shorter than he, she blared her tuba voice in his direction.

When she'd got accepted as a Junior String Project scholarship student, he'd asked, "How come you picked the cello?"

"It sounds the best of all the instruments."

"How'd you decide that?"

"I listened at the string recital and it made me happy every time the cello came in."

"It's as big as you are."

"You're thinking about the bass. That's the big one."

"Robin the head cheerleader played the bass."

She'd giggled. "Now you're teasing me, Karl. If she'd played the bass, you wouldn't be here now, I bet."

"Smarty."

Like all smokers who've quit smoking, Karl chewed the end of his pen when he was with clients, and a wad of gum when he wasn't. The sound of his jaws and the killer air-conditioning in his Honda made a little white noise for us as he drove down the service road, along the one through street out of Old Metairie, across the railroad track, over the bayou. We pulled into a cul-de-sac in a neighborhood that, although just a stone's throw, just a crow's flight, away from ours, might as well have been in another parish. The homes were larger, the lots were deeper and with established plantings, but the property taxes were half, the asking prices less, and the schools worse. Also the houses looked entirely different from the small pastel cottages or the one-room-wide shotguns in our old, enclosed area. They all had one-story fronts and large two-story backs that looked like add-ons.

"How come?" I asked Karl about that, as we disembarked on the sidewalk in the heavy heat.

"When these houses were built," he explained, getting out his octopus of realtor's keys, "they were taxed on the number of windows on the front. So you put the major square-footage on the back. This used to be a settlement of well-to-do merchants; then, after the end of World War Two, it began to go downhill. Now it's on the rise." He showed me the names of previous owners: Jacques Goudchaux, Simon Herrman, Alf Brown. "Now we've got tri-racial and they all put up British coats of arms in their family rooms."

Workmen had taken the weekend off, but left all their gear. Outside, we passed a Pot O'Gold portapotty; inside, drop cloths, ladders, sanders, paint cans. Rugs lay rolled in the wide entry hall and framed portraits of children sat stacked on the floor.

Karl led me up the curving stairway to a bedroom shaded by cottonwood trees. "This used to be the nursery, I think. Maybe later, the mother-in-law's room? If I had it, I'd use it for an office. Nice space."

"This bedroom would hold half my house."

"Location," he said. "Bad schools, big lots." He folded his sunglasses into his pocket and stuck his gum on the edge of the windowsill. He gestured to me to come with him. "Look here," he said, reaching something down from a high shelf in a bare double closet. "I left this where I found it. I wanted you to see." He handed me a letter. "Check the date."

I read the neat penmanship on faint blue paper:

Miss Louisa Blancet
Miss Jayne Atkins
Miss Theodora Talley
  Within three days send five copies of this letter,
leaving off the top name and adding your name to the

*bottom. Send a hanky to each of the above names. Pin
your name and address to each hanky. You will receive
fifty-five hankies—if the chain isn't broken. You will
start receiving hankies right away.*

It's fun to see where the hankies come from.

Yours for fun,

The Hanky Club

DECEMBER 7, 1941

Tears stung my eyes. The letter reminded me of my
mother. Of her drawer of ironed handkerchiefs: hem-
stitched, lace-trimmed, embroidered, scalloped. She would
have been—thirteen. Off in East Texas, starting, perhaps, a
hope chest, learning what was expected of females. I had an
image of her, a girl like her, with rich auburn hair and pale
skin, sending off a letter to her friends on what we came to
know, from school, as Pearl Harbor Day. The outside world,
the coming war, bad things, not a part of her life.

A *nice* letter—in a not-nice world.

"Is this for me?" I asked, wiping my eyes on my T-shirt
sleeve.

"Sure." Karl looked pleased, his square German face
turning a little red. "I thought since you fancied those old
roses, well, this seemed to fit in. I thought you'd get off
to it."

"I do." I sniffled. The flimsy blue stationery, which I
tucked in my shorts pocket, made me think of my sister.
How there had been a time when I'd have called her with
this first thing. Asking, "Do you think our mother sent one
like this?" "Of course she did, I bet she did, I know she did,

let's ask her," my sister, when she was young, when we were close, would have answered.

Sometimes, like today, when Birdie stood in her old-fashioned cello-playing dress, sturdy legs apart, chin thrust forward, eating her veggie sandwich, music still in her head, I would remember Terrell. How Terrell had been at that age, such a serious pianist, no makeup, glasses sliding down the bridge of her nose, chewing on her lower lip, making great fortissimo sounds come from our parents' rebuilt upright piano. Before she became the blond, beautiful, perfect daughter.

"Unnh—," I sniffled.

"Does this mean I at least get a cup of coffee?"

I dug a crumpled Kleenex from my pocket. "Maybe we can scrape together enough for an alien movie."

5

Dear Mother,

Daddy said on the phone last week that you wanted to have all of your grandchildren together for your birthday. What a fine idea, and we are delighted to be included.

I hope you are bearing up under the dreadful heat and dry skies. We've had high winds and battering rains, as I'm sure you've read about. A tropical storm, they are careful to call it, since hurricane season is not considered to begin until August. This weather is very hard on outdoor gardens, but I have covered my roses with tarps and hope this will blow over, so that I may bring you a bouquet when I come. I wish I could bring some of the rain also.

Enclosed is a long-ago chain letter a friend of mine shared with me; her mother found it stuck in an old photo album. It made me wonder if you had any letters saved from those days or from after the war, perhaps from your courtship with Daddy. Wouldn't the grandchildren love to see them?

*I am hoping to find a sleeveless linen dress for your
celebration, perhaps in the lemony yellow I know you
like.*

> *Love,*
>
> *Ella*

ONE VIOLET LANE
OLD METAIRIE

'd taken Birdie's suggestion—in fact I had also taken Birdie—and combed through the dresses at the secondhand shop in the Pink Mall, but it was a consignment shop, everything what I'd call resort wear, Florida clothes: sweaters with appliquéd flowers over matching floral-print silk dresses. Not for me. Only the people who sold them would want to buy them.

Then I looked under *Thrifts* in the Yellow Pages, finding a Recycle, a Salvation Army Store, a Second Hand Roze, and one called Your Turn, which appeared to be connected to the old Episcopal church that I had pretended to attend with Terrell. Second Hand Roze had clothes I would have sold my clunky Chevy for: long skirts made of tissue-thin cotton, skinny cotton tops stitched at the neck and sleeves, in black and navy and claret, classy things you could wear all year in our climate. But to what? And with whom? To water my houses? To talk to Birdie's cello teacher? To eat popcorn on the fourth row of an indie film with Karl, who always parked his gum under the seat? But at Your Turn, there was the dress I needed. It wasn't yellow, it was a tad too long for daytime styles (better than too short), and about a size too big. But, hey. It was a celadon green, the only flaw a slight faded streak across the shoulders in the back. Brief sleeves and a ribbon-edged collar. A dress begging (in vain) for pearls. My daughter got an elephant-gray jumper, tie back, buttons down the front, in a size made for someone at least six feet tall. So big it looked as if it had a dropped waist.

"You can't wear that," I said. "It swallows you."

"Felice's mom can cut it off. She sews. And Grandmom will love it."

"Why?"

"Because it's not something, you know, I would ever buy myself, so she'll think you bought it for me."

"Jeez—" What had I done to deserve such a child?

Tonight, with Birdie done with her practicing, on the phone to Felice and brushing out her damp Botticelli mass of hair, I sat on my bed in the dark, listening to the steady beating rain. My tenant, the schoolteacher, went off to stay on the Virginia shore with her parents for the months of July and August. She still paid rent—to hold her half of the duplex—and she didn't run up any utility bills, which I paid. But I still had to check on her place, make sure the flooding wasn't messing up the plumbing, that there weren't leaks, that there wasn't water seeping in some- where, ruining rugs or clothes. Summer hurricanes when she was gone were all mine to handle; so were the ones in September when she was here.

I'd spooked myself, thinking about planes being grounded, about bad weather, planes getting caught in an updraft or a downdraft or in the squalling winds. Maybe we shouldn't fly after all? I tried to read, to look through my antique-rose catalogues, to fall asleep, but I kept seeing my sister in that little Piper Cherokee, its wings icing up in the sudden sleet.

She'd called me the week before she left to tell me, "I'm going out to meet him in Notrees, I actually am, Mr. Emu. I can't keep putting him off. He wants us to, you know, get together. To tell everybody. And I want that, too, I think." She sounded excited, keyed up, uncertain.

I'd been happy at the sound of her voice, thinking this a Christmas call, a part of me wishing we were going to be in Austin with the rest of them, a larger part of me glad that I wouldn't have been able to come even if I'd been invited. From before Christmas to Mardi Gras was my second-busiest season. Skiers packed up their whole families and headed out to Colorado. Plants had to be coddled through changeable weather—from almost warm to suddenly bitter and biting—and less natural light in the shorter days.

It took me a few seconds to grasp what she was saying, to understand her words. "You mean leave Red?"

"I don't know, Ella." Her voice lifted. "Maybe."

"You really love this guy."

"We're crazy about each other, but we never have time. You know? I guess I'm going out there to find out. You think, when you get together with someone on the quiet, the way I did with him, that it's going to be time out from the stuff you do every day. But it isn't. I feel like we became lovers, and then all of a sudden we're dealing with summer camps and car inspections and root canals. We might as well be married. Not really, but I mean what you want with

someone new is to forget all that daily business you get farther and farther behind in, like the Whatever Stables, where
you shovel it half as fast as they make it. I know it's been
rough this year out there in Notrees, but that's all we talk
about. It's been a rough year here, too, if you get down to it,
with Rufus having a midlife. But when I take off my Wonder
Bra and panties, I want to zone out and just, pardon me,
fuck my mind blank. But it doesn't work that way. He talks
about how it'll take five years to grow back the beef they
sold to slaughter. How they'll have to put down the emus,
too, if the drought drags on. Sometimes when we're
together he doesn't even take his boots off, much less his
pants. He just sits and talks. We've got to get away, to have
some time."

"What will you tell everybody? The folks—and Red?"

"I'm saying there's a Mexican furniture mart in Odessa.
Who'll ever check?"

"Maybe you'd like to really come see me this time, to get
away and think about it?" Although it panicked me, the idea
that she actually might, I meant it.

She didn't answer right away. Then she said, "You know
Mom and Dad still have that pitiful upright."

"That you used to play."

"Well, it really got to me over there at Christmas. 'Oh,
Terrell will play the carols for us, won't you, honey?' That's
all they ever wanted, me to show off when they had company. It was another social skill, like ballet or tennis or sailing. Forget being serious about music."

"You were good," I told her.

"Was I?"

"You practiced all the time."

"Mother used to tell me it was ruining my posture. She just wanted the end results."

"You were good," I repeated.

"I don't know if I was or not. Anyway, it's too late now." She forced a laugh. "Did you see this article in the paper, you must've, AP wire or whatever, how one in every eight plant species is under threat? These botanists around the world spent *thirty years* working on a Red List of Imperiled Plants. I mean these people who are saving whales and owls forget it's the plants that convert sunlight to food for us to eat. I sent them a donation, some conservancy. But you know what I thought, Ella? I thought I'd give every single thing I have, including, maybe even including, Mr. Emu, to have spent thirty years of my life working on *one single thing.* You know?"

"I do," I said. And I thought of Henry, the head rose gardener at Belle Vue, who really did what I only pretended to do.

"Honest"—Terrell finished up the call—"I owe you one, for listening to all this stuff and not telling a soul. Maybe I *will* come for real one of these days. See that fancy pink house of yours and eat in that French place you wrote me about." And she sounded like she almost meant it.

I'd found myself thinking about that call a lot lately, probably because I was going back home again. Taking myself to task because somehow I hadn't done something: begged her not to go, got her to postpone the trip. But naturally I didn't, because I knew she wanted me to understand and be on her side, and cover for her if she needed it, if she didn't want to come back. Still, I wondered what all that had done to Red, and if he knew, or what he knew, and how he was handling not having had a chance to work it out.

You never knew what went wrong with other people's marriages. I couldn't have pinpointed the minute things went sour with Buddy and me, when bed wasn't enough. Maybe if I'd had more sense—but then if I'd had more sense, I wouldn't have come to Louisiana with some hunk of a guy I didn't really know, expecting everything to work out the way it was supposed to in your life. But if I could have picked one marriage and called it perfect, it would have been Terrell and Red's. She'd waited so long to be sure, and he'd waited so long for her to say yes. If any two people should have known each other, they were the ones.

Besides, how could she find anybody more decent or easier to be with than Red Hall had been? At least when I knew him best. And I couldn't believe that just because he'd got to be R. Rufus Hall, attorney-at-law, he'd changed into someone else. He seemed the same kind of accepting guy he'd always been the few times I'd seen him since I left town. I remembered when I went back pregnant with Birdie, trying not to react to the way Mother looked anywhere but at my bulging middle, the way she carefully did not mention what she could see with her own eyes, Red had come in and right away given me a squeeze, and said he hoped it was a girl and that their little boys, then two and three, could sure use a cousin. I remembered the two of us, Red and I, sat on the sunporch at Mother's while everyone else busied themselves with the festive birthday meal. We'd watched the boys, Borden and Bailey, run about in their Sunday rompers, and talked about nothing much.

He'd had a way, in his law school days, of pulling off his glasses and rubbing the corner of his eyes with his knuckles, if he was concentrating, or putting them on top of his head, jamming them in his mop of hair, if he was talking to you and wanted to see your eyes. It made me smile, that visit, how he would reach a hand up to his temple, realize nothing was there, and shake his head, as if just remembering he had contacts, then lean his arms on his knees and clasp his hands. "Maybe we ought to take these two rowdies out for a Blue Bell Supreme ice cream cone," he'd suggested, knowing, I guess, that nothing tasted better to a woman with a gnawing stomach than ice cream. But then Daddy had come in to say brunch was ready. And Terrell, still looking like a Bluebonnet Belle at thirty-two, had rounded up her sons. While Mother suggested to me, "Perhaps you'd like to freshen up before we eat, dear."

Of course, not being around them, Red and my sister, except on those rare weekends home, where the subtexts of my return overpowered any attempt to sit and talk, I didn't know how they were really doing. I did watch them once, from the doorway of my parents' house, on a later visit, standing by their late-model Volvo, having what looked to be a fight. This was five years ago, when I'd been more or less reinstated as acceptable because of my changed status to "widow." The boys, then twelve and thirteen, had waited on the sidewalk, hands in their Sunday trouser pockets, looking around casually, as if they weren't overhearing their parents argue. Red was leaning with his back against the passenger door, facing the house, his arms folded across his chest, looking defensive. My sister, angry, moved her mouth and flung her arms in the air in frustration. When she abruptly turned her back to him, I could see her wipe her eyes and straighten the belt on her sleeveless saffron linen dress. Then she gathered the boys together and hurried them all into the house.

"Hello, Ella." Red spoke in that easy way he always had, as if he'd just seen me yesterday. "You're looking good."

"Hey, sweetie." Terrell had given me a hasty hug, her eyes glittery with recent tears. "We were just having a family conference. Too much weekend company, I think. I'm frayed at the edges." She held me at arm's length, checking me out. "You look good. Blue's your color."

Still, it never dawned on me that the two of them might be having real trouble, serious trouble. Couples had words by the car just the same as they had words in the backyard or the bedroom. That was the nature of living together. It hadn't occurred to me that Terrell might really mean to leave him.

"Be careful," I'd told her on that January phone call. And I guess I wasn't thinking of her plane ride.

✳ Austin

6

It seemed strange, waiting on my parents' porch like a caller, a visitor, a bouquet of old roses in my arms. I felt homesick, if not exactly for the yellow frame two-story, my growing-up home, then for the girls my sister and I had been here. For the time when we were the children of this house in its familiar, settled neighborhood west of downtown, on a limestone bluff above a creek.

Henry had cut and wrapped for me a selection of his finest roses, an armful of almost unbearable fragrance and melting hues. I held them as an offering.

"Aren't you going to ring the doorbell?" Birdie asked. "Mom?"

I stood, hesitating in the harsh heat. "Yes," I told her, and I did. I rang the doorbell of my mother's house.

Daddy welcomed us inside, dressed as he always was at home, in a pressed blue dress shirt (damp across his back), long khaki pants (damp across the seat from working all day at his desk), house slippers with felt insides.

"Guten Tag," he said, hurrying us into the cool hallway.

"Bonjour." I kissed his whiskered cheek. He looked older, more stooped, as if the wind had been knocked out of his sails. Perhaps I hadn't been too observant in January at the funeral.

Birdie stood to one side, lugging the strapped suitcase we shared. Because direct flights between New Orleans and Austin were scarce, we'd opted to fly through Houston, two short hops on Southwest Airlines, and so packed for an overnight visit.

"You're supposed to say 'Hi,' " Daddy told her, winking and taking the heavy bag.

"Hi," she said agreeably.

"Your mother will be along shortly, Ella." He moved us into the living room. "Sorry to make you girls take a cab, but our old bones and our old car in this heat—"

"Did you know I play the cello, Granddaddy?" Birdie asked him, grabbing his elbow to get his attention. "In the String Project?"

"I believe I heard that."

"My mom says you have a lot of music. Can I see?"

"Well, now, let's have a look. I might happen to have a few CDs to your liking." He led her along. "Your mother reports you've made a change in your name."

"Robin is still my real name, but my friends and everybody call me Birdie, because that's what I like."

"What do you reckon they call you at your granddad's house?"

Birdie giggled. She looked up (half a mile) at my daddy, and, imitating his pitch exactly, boomed, " 'Hey, Girlie.' "

Daddy laughed out loud, something I hadn't seen in years, and, putting a hand on her shoulder, led her into his book-lined library.

Left alone, I felt rooted to the spot, short of breath. I peeled back the tissue paper so the roses could breathe. The living room seemed to be someone else's. I felt the way you do waiting in a school friend's house, looking all around at the matching stuff, wondering what it would be like to live in a place like this, what people who lived like this *did*, what they said to one another. The paired green chairs, the facing flowered sofas, the matted bird prints behind non-glare glass, the egg-yolk-yellow walls, the apple-green rug. Had I really lived here?

My cradled roses, each cupped and sumptuous bloom as old as history, in here seemed faded, shabby.

"My dear," my mother murmured, sweeping into the bright room, wearing an appliquéd cotton sweater over a green shell and slim slacks. "I'm sorry not to be here the moment—I assumed you had your bags to wait for, and the awful taxicab ride your dad insisted on . . ."

"How nice you look," I said, handing her the roses.

"Why, what's this?" She brightened and pecked my cheek. "From your garden, Ella. Isn't that thoughtful. We haven't had enough flowers to—I quite gave up on my azaleas this spring." She held the bouquet away from her and headed for the kitchen in search of a vase. "Perhaps in the guest bath? I have pink guest towels somewhere." She peered at me while she put them in tap water. "I suppose shorts do make sense

in this heat. But on an airplane—? Well, your generation—"
She studied the effect, frowned, and headed for the
small guest bathroom that I remembered as cloying in its
mingled scents of the soaps and sachets to which professors'
wives fell heir. "Where's your girl?" she asked when she
returned.

"She's with Daddy in the library. They're talking music."

Tears came to my mother's eyes. "Did you know this,
Ella? *Robin* was the name your sister liked the best. I'm sure
if she'd had a daughter . . . She used to ask me, when she
was just a little thing, could she change her name to Robin?
I'd always scold her: *Terrell* is a good family name." She
pinched her nose with her fingers and smoothed the line
between her eyes. "What could it have mattered?"

"She's called Birdie in school."

"Well, a nickname like that won't last, now will it?" She
called toward the open doorway. "Judah?"

Daddy came at once, with my daughter in tow. "Agatha,
do you recall that our granddaughter plays the cello?"

Mother nodded, still shaken. "Terrell, you remember,
had a fine proficiency at the piano by that age. Musical talent
runs in our family." She squinted at Birdie. "Did you have all
that hair the last time you were here? I can't think . . . it
must be dreadfully hot."

While I stood there, trying to keep my anger in check,
Birdie walked up to her grandmother and held out her
hand. "My mom and I always pull our hair back for public
occasions. I imagine you used to do that." She stared up at
my mother's cropped, once-auburn hair, now a mix of cin-
namon and tan.

"Well, Robin," Mother said, "I believe that perhaps while you are visiting here . . ."

"She wants a nickname," my daddy said, "then Birdie it is." He offered the opinion that young people were not so pre-occupied with names as many of the older generation. "My dad," he told my daughter, "gave me and my brother Bible names, strong names with a prophecy to them. Take Judah, my name, he's the one people will gather round and praise. Take my brother, Reuben, he's the one given dignity and power. Now is it any surprise I turned out to be a teacher, and my brother a judge back in Ector County? And Agatha, your grandmother, she plucked names from her family tree—Terrell and Ellis—though we softened that one a bit when your mama came along, another girl, called her Ella."

Sitting on the glassed-in porch that looked out on Mother's yard, I could see a few things blooming—yellow rudbeckia, blue plumbago, red geraniums—but the beds, usually a quilt of summer blooms, looked depleted, and the stone birdbath, baking. Under the glare of the blistering afternoon sun, the watered grass had turned brown on top.

Mother began a story, one of her yard stories. Her way of putting a bit of distance between herself and us. This one involved a crow, not as frequent a visitor to her garden, she said, as the mockingbird. She leaned toward us, a tall woman, trim, turning seventy, her legs crossed, one foot swinging slightly. "There he was, waddling the way crows do, like penguins, their wide-apart gait, going right up to this squirrel who was eating the leftover biscuit I'd put out by the hibiscus. Retreating, walking around, in that side-ways way they have, then coming right up to the pesky squirrel and doing just what I'd have liked to do myself, poking him, sharp as a needle, with his beak—"

Daddy brought us a tea party, iced spiced tea with orange slices and a plate of wafer-thin ginger cookies. "I'm working on walking again," he allowed, setting the tray down in slow motion. "I read in the Tufts Health Letter that walking shoes are no help to folks in my decade. That the trouble is, the thick, spongy soles that are supposed to cushion your feet only make you unsteady. I'm going to take their advice and buy myself some leather shoes with hard rubber soles."

I could think of nothing to say. I drained my iced tea. Birdie had a third cookie. "What time are they coming tomorrow?" I asked. I didn't know what to call my sister's family, afraid to say her name.

"I told Rufus to bring my grandsons about eleven," Mother replied evenly. "A daytime event, because of the young people. Your dad suggested this get-together, having the idea that I should be photographed with all my grandchildren this year." She rose abruptly and began to collect our spiced-tea glasses on the tray.

"Will they stay on in their house?" I asked, wondering if I should have said *her house, Terrell's house*. With Borden, the older boy, going off to college next year, and Bailey, the next, I thought my sister's fine home might seem too large, too empty.

"Now that you mention the matter," Daddy began, "they already made some changes. Before she—"

"No need to go into all that at this time, Judah," Mother snapped. She looked through the glass at the dry yard. "I cannot understand how we can have a humidity in the sixties day after day, as if we were on Galveston Island, with a temperature reaching a hundred and not a drop of rain condensing out. Can you tell me why on earth they can't seed the clouds?"

"Mother," I suggested, trying to offer them an outing, "we didn't bring you a proper birthday present, but Birdie and I would like to take you and Daddy out for Mexican food tonight."

"Oh." Mother almost dropped the tray. "The last time we went, with Terrell—" She shut her eyes, blinked.

"How about the Spanish Village, Agatha? We haven't tried that for years." Daddy looked pleased at the idea, perked up. To me he said, "Remember how we used to go when you were a little thing, Ella, and you'd eat the deluxe dinner right down to the bare plate?"

Mother steadied herself. "We could do that," she agreed. She smoothed her face with effort. To me, she said, "You two might want to take a little rest, dear, unpack and clean up, perhaps change from your shorts. You must be tired after your trip." Her gaze speaking louder than words: How was she to bear it that this daughter, the wrong daughter, was here on her porch, while her favorite, her firstborn, was gone?

7

The next morning, Sunday, dressing for Mother's birthday brunch in the large double room I had once shared, I kept glimpsing Terrell instead of my daughter in front of the full-length mirror. My sister as she had been as a schoolgirl, so serious, brushing her fine, light hair, music going on in her head (as it must now be with Birdie). Sometimes Terrell would hum, without being aware of it, or tap her fingers on the dressing table. I could see the back of her, across the blue carpet, straight legs, straight spine, listening attentively to what I couldn't hear. And then—where did that girl go? My sister a sweetheart nominee in high school, a Bluebonnet Belle in the university, molting into a lawyer's wife with a sailing club. Maybe she'd run off, as I had, but in a different way.

My secondhand celadon linen dress greened my spirits. How could my mother not be delighted with it? I put on my face, took an aspirin, and brushed my damp brown tangles into some sort of shape.

Birdie had cut off the ties of her elephant-gray jumper, and used one piece to pull her own waterfall of hair back into a thick ponytail. The dress itself (shortened by Felice's mom) fell to her ankles, cool and proper, in the style of a storybook girl from the last century, complete with Chinese slippers (borrowed from Felice), black and strapped, the modern Mary Janes.

"I guess Grandma is having a hard time getting over losing Aunt Terrell."

I looked past my daughter into the mirror. "You don't get over something like that. You just wear it down or it wears you down."

"I guess you'd have a hard time, wouldn't you, if I died like that?"

"I'd tear my hair out by the roots, is what."

She made a shy smile and looked away. "Maybe Grand-mom tore some out."

"Maybe she did," I said, and smothered my daughter in a hug for her charity.

I would have been absolutely crawling out of my skin with nerves at the idea of one of these red-letter, special-event birthday parties, if it hadn't been for the fact that Red would be here. Someone from the past, who'd not only known me when I was that earlier version of me that my mother still couldn't forgive, but had known us all, the whole family, for over half my life, and his, too. He must have been around, we all must have—he and Terrell, Buddy and I—for Mother's forty-fifth birthday. Was that possible? Her ever being the age I was fast approaching? That he and Terrell had already reached? Young, she must have been, my mother, then. And different? Or (sad thought) the same?

It would be good to see the boys, too. All I recalled from the funeral, the lot of us in shock, was them suddenly grown, in dark suits, polite, shaking everyone's hands, their faces stricken. Not the young, stringy kids I remembered from my last birthday visit home (me, a fresh widow, back in favor), waiting on the sidewalk, hands jammed into pockets, while their parents quarreled. I knew the older boy, Borden, would be going off to Yale this fall—good news my sister had not lived to hear. And that Bailey, the younger one, had a number of the attributes of second siblings: not quite as many accomplishments, grades not quite as stellar, and the look of expecting that somehow he'd done something wrong. A look I'd seen often enough in the mirror.

"Now that's nice, dear," Mother said when Birdie and I came downstairs, taking in my linen dress, my pale hose and summer sandals. With the smallest of frowns, she reached up and pushed my still-damp hair into shape. "And you, too, Robin. Did you know—my girls used to wear just such jumpers?" Her voice caught.

"Mom bought it for me, Grandmother, in the Pink Mall, for your birthday."

"Well. Isn't that fine." She stared at my daughter as if she were some rector's child or young professor's daughter, someone to be kindly toward. Composed, readied for the event, for turning seventy in the presence of family, she wore a silk dress in her favorite pale yellow with a double strand of pearls. Early this morning, she'd slipped out of the house and got her hair done, so that it now shone with auburn highlights. She turned to me. "Ella, I put those flowers from your garden out on the sunporch. They looked as if they could use a little light. Or fresh water? I'm sure you wrote me the names of several of them; I hope you'll forgive me, I'm a bit distracted."

"Of course," I assured her. "Roses don't travel well, even with the stems in tubes. I only wanted—" What had I wanted? I might as well have brought a homemade, misshapen birthday cake that she needed to pretend to appreciate. Past her head, on the dining table with its white linen cloth, I saw an arrangement of yellow florist's daffodils and green lemon leaves. My roses belonged to another world; here, their fragrance disappeared, as the smell of a peach in an aroma shop. "Your own flowers are doing well in this heat and drought," I told her. "That's your green thumb."

"I try," she said, looking past me to the glass-walled porch and the yard beyond. "I do try."

Then I heard the doorbell and rushed out into the hall in time to see Daddy clapping Red and the two grandsons on the shoulder, saying, "Come in, come in." He'd got himself in a fresh sky-blue shirt and tie, and had put on leather shoes instead of his felt-lined bedroom slippers. "Good, good, you brought your camera, Rufus. Ours has been acting up. We haven't taken many, I guess you understand, in recent months."

"*Red,*" I said, restraining myself from throwing my arms around him. "Gosh, I'm glad to see you."

"Hello, Ella." He looked glad, too, taking my hand in both of his. "How are you?"

"Did you remember I'm called Birdie now?" my daughter asked the boys, who towered above her.

"Yeah." The younger one smoothed down his cowlick,

which stood straight up. He wore a dress shirt for the event that didn't quite fit (the neck too big, the sleeves too long), probably a hand-me-down from his brother. "Yeah. Dad said." But he didn't look too sure.

Wanting to show my nephews I was glad to see them, which I was, I held out my hand to each in turn, hesitant to try a hug. "Hello, Bailey," I said. "Hello, Barnum."

"Borden." The older boy gave me a vexed look. His fair hair was slicked back, Gatsby-style, and he was as tall as my daddy, a basketball star and brain, with his mom's good looks.

I tapped my head to indicate I was losing it. All of us, it was clear, under strain.

Mother greeted them, then turned, as if overwhelmed by the proximity of all her remaining family. "Shall we go in?" she requested. "I believe we're ready to serve."

She had got the woman who sometimes cooked for her (she never called it *catering*) to make chicken crêpes and a lemon and raspberry mousse cake. She'd baked her own special sweet-milk biscuits and delegated the soft-scrambled eggs to Daddy. "Eggs are back," he explained, quoting from one of his many health letters. "Butter, too. You see how they demolished oleo in the paper? Guys on low-fat diets get more strokes." He took care, too, of the drinks: orange juice for everyone, coffee for the adults and Borden, green tea for Birdie and Bailey, a glass of white wine for Mother. He'd poured it for her, not asking (since she would have thought it proper to demur), saying a person ought to celebrate with a little spirits on her birthday.

The meal went all right; the food was delicious (certainly

a treat for me), and Daddy did most of the talking, about how their good habits were responsible for Mother's looking not even old enough to have grandchildren at seventy. And about how fortunate they were, however, to have all of theirs on hand for this milestone. How, by his eightieth, his grandsons might be thinking of starting families of their own. The boys rolled their eyes. Birdie giggled. "I guess you'll have to be ninety before I'm ready, Granddaddy."

Mostly everything went fine because Red was so wonderful with my parents. The way he'd always been. I remembered back to when he first started coming around, after he and Terrell had begun to go out occasionally. The whole structure of the law, or the Law, as Daddy spoke of it with awe, was based on precedent: what had the courts done in the past; how could that be interpreted, or cited, or stretched in the present case? It seemed natural for him to talk with my daddy about history, since precedence was just another name for the history of legal decisions. Daddy would expound until it made your ears ring and your eyes glaze over about the differences between British law and American law, between the cultures that created the different systems. And Red never got tired of that or ran out of questions. "Good boy you've got there," my daddy began to tell Terrell. Or, "Where's that young man of yours? We haven't seen him lately."

With Mother, Red had been equally engaging. His family had been around since the start of Texas, dirt farmers north and east of town in a little wide spot on the road called Pflugerville. His mom had been a vocational nurse (though he didn't mention that she'd quit nursing by the time he met

Terrell and was working in a dry cleaner's shop). His dad, he said, was a builder. Which sounded better than saying that he got and lost at least a dozen jobs a year helping contractors put up their houses, lost them because everything he tried to do ended up undone. Any nail he drove, Red used to confide, went in crooked; any leak in the roof became two leaks when he tried to patch it. But, nonetheless, it wasn't a lie to say that his family had been pioneers in Central Texas, the Halls. He'd mention that, then get Mother to talking about her kin in East Texas, the Adams clan, that was her maiden name, the Terrells, the Ellises, for whom my sister and I were named. How rich the farmland was there, how, yes, they'd had dairy farms just the same as Red's great-grandparents, whose farm was not ten miles from the present Blue Bell Supreme creamery. How, yes, it did give you a feel for the land. Her very tone conjuring up the landed gentry of another century. "That nice young man called," she began to say to Terrell. "Tell me his name again."

Today, Red made a festive flattering production out of photographing Mother with her three grandchildren. Setting up his camera on a tripod, moving chairs out onto the sunporch, deciding there was too much glare, moving them back into the living room, careful not to have the high school photos of Terrell and me in the background, arranging the chairs in front of the framed paned birds. "Not easy to get you and all your flock in one shot," he told her, reminding her of the many who were present. Not mentioning the one who was gone.

Still, it couldn't have been easy for her, blowing out her seven yellow dripless tapers, smiling as everyone sang, touching Daddy's hand as he toasted his bride of more than forty-five years. Any way you arranged it, this year was different.

In the past, every year for Mother's birthday, the three of us posed for a formal portrait, Mother in the center, a daughter on each side. A ritual that had begun when I was a toddler, Terrell starting kindergarten. We did this annually until I ran off with Buddy and Terrell became engaged to Red. After that, because I seldom returned, not exactly welcome, and because we were grown and so one year looked a lot like the last, we began to take marker shots on Mother's major birthdays: when she turned fifty, and I was still helping Buddy repo yachts and Terrell was helping R. Rufus Hall make partner; fifty-five, when Terrell had her boys, and I was pregnant with Birdie, no husband in sight, and so happy I hardly minded that no one wanted to see me; sixty, when we first got the three cousins together; sixty-five, when I, the sudden widow, was welcome once again. Photos showing Terrell and me growing taller, older, altering in various ways; photos showing Mother at the center, never changing.

Daddy had come up with the idea to begin afresh, this time with the grandchildren, who would one day be turning into adults, taking spouses, having young, providing them a wonderful certain increase in numbers.

"Are you ready, Agatha?" Red asked, when his gear was set up.

"Yes, certainly." She straightened her yellow neckline, adjusted her pearls, smoothed the line between her eyes. "Whenever you are, Rufus."

After trying a shot or two with everyone seated, Red

moved the chairs away and tried them standing. He'd taken off his navy linen jacket, and worked in white shirtsleeves (though not rolled above the elbows, the way he had in the old days), his Canon camera now in his hand. When he leaned over, I could see scattered white in his well-cut dark hair. He first posed them as stairsteps: Borden, Bailey, Agatha, Birdie. Then, taking his time, he tried another grouping, this time with Mother and Birdie facing out at the center, a tall boy on either side, like bookends. Coaxing smiles, he said, "Say *rain please.*" He fidgeted with the focus. "Hmmm," he said, "let's try this." He sat Mother in a chair and had the grandchildren cluster around her, each down on one knee, so no tall teen head rose above hers. So that everyone looked at her. "Say *the queen's knees,*" he instructed. And at that my mother blushed a little and tugged at the hem of her yellow silk dress, then glanced up at him with a sudden flirty look, which the camera caught.

A fine first photo for a new album.

8

Red and I sat on the air-cooled porch, and even with the deep overhang of the roof, I was still aware of the baking midday sun. While my parents cleaned up the kitchen, in their own way, taking their time, and our children sprawled in the living room, getting reacquainted, I took a moment to lay my roses to rest in Mother's yard. Removing the Belle Vue bouquet from its unwelcoming cut-glass vase, I spread the blooms to dry beneath an Indian-yellow rudbeckia. Closing the door against the heat on my return.

Red loosened his tie and shoes, emitting a deep sigh he more than likely wasn't aware of, and stretched his legs in front of him. "Did you bring those?" he asked.

I pressed my hand to my chest bone because it still hurt, carrying them all this way, a gesture, having them treated like roadside weeds. "On the plane, for her birthday." I didn't need to say anything more.

He and I used to sit out here on the porch this way, easy together, talking, or not talking, mostly waiting. In those days, he'd be waiting for Terrell to come downstairs or to come in from class, or, sometimes, even from another date, if it had to do with a social function at the university. I mostly waited on Buddy to show up, for by that time he'd given up on her and started hanging around me, taking me out (when Mother thought I was going with friends), us doing most everything we could in the car, him letting me out at the corner to walk home, blue jeans rumpled, lipstick gone, hair a wild mess. Sometimes I'd be cooling off, sitting out here with Red, wondering how it was you ran away from home. In those days, Mother's azalea beds stopped traffic in the spring. And, if it was late afternoon, we'd sit and hear cars braking, and see people getting out to take pictures.

"You want to get a hamburger?" Red would sometimes ask me, if it didn't look like Terrell was coming back anytime soon, or if he was in low spirits about how she kept him guessing.

"Sure," I always said. He probably didn't have any money to be buying me burgers, but in those days I didn't understand that. I thought every guy in his twenties came with a wallet, with money he somehow made, and that girls like me, still in high school, with parents who wanted them to concentrate on studying, came flat broke except for what their daddies gave them. How could I have been so dumb? Was that something families like ours did to keep their girls at home till they married? Here Birdie was already making spending money baby- and cat-sitting, counting the months till she could have an after-school job to buy herself a proper cello. At her age I hadn't so much as rolled a burrito behind the counter at Taco Bell.

Going off in the car with Red—a law student—gave me a big charge. We'd always go to this ratty drive-up place near campus, supposed to have the best burgers at the lowest price. I'd always get a chiliburger with cheese, and he'd get the one with the special hickory sauce and onions. Sometimes he'd have a beer, but I always got a Coke, mostly because Daddy wouldn't let us keep soft drinks at home (I guess he'd already, way back then, been reading up on health). Then I'd lean back against the passenger door of Red's very used old Peugeot, and tuck my feet up, so we could really get down to talking. I loved those times. It felt like a date, almost, and I'd be wiping the chili off my face and feeling excited—because being alone with someone in a car was intimate, it just was—and then, every time, he'd lean close, the longneck beer bottle in his hand, all that dark curly hair falling over his forehead, hazel eyes looking through horn-rims and he'd ask me, "You think she'll ever marry a mutt like me?"

That's what I was for him, the kid sister. The one it didn't matter what you talked to about. He'd go on about his dad, who was still alive and driving him crazy, because his mom was getting fed up with having to bail him out. Or he'd talk about his classes, which he loved, how one day he was going to use the law to fix a few things out there that needed fixing.

A couple of times I did the inviting. "You got time for a hamburger? In your car?" I'd ask. And then I would buy the burger, from my allowance, because I really needed his advice or just needed to let off steam, about how I meant to get away from here, somehow. Get away before my parents washed my brain the way they had my sister's, though of course I didn't say that to him. The last time we went out I had to ask him some legal advice. After making sure he knew I wasn't pregnant. We were in his crammed-full car, with him leaning against the driver's door, the seat pushed back so he could eat without the steering wheel in the way. "I'm going to run off and get married," I told him. "This is between you and me, period; nobody else, especially not my sister, especially not my parents, is supposed to hear about this. When I'm gone, you didn't know a thing about it. 'Ella?' you're going to say, 'I haven't seen her in weeks.' 'Ella?' you're going to say, 'how would I know?' But you need to tell me what to do. We're going to Louisiana. Buddy's got a job, hot job, he says. He says he's not going without me."

The gist of Red's advice was to get our license in Austin, wait our three days, get our blood tests, get a J.P., and then, when it was a done deal, head across the state line. He didn't know Louisiana law, but it was different. It might be easy, even easier. He'd heard that in some state in the South, you could marry at fifteen, even cousins, but that was hearsay. I was in college, nineteen, Buddy was twenty-two. Here there'd be no problem. And that's just what we did, what he said. By the time word got out, we were legal and eating fried catfish at a motel on the Vermilion River outside Lafayette.

I never thanked Red properly, since the next time I saw him was at his and Terrell's wedding, to which I'd been invited because how could she not have her sister? And that didn't seem the time, what with all that white satin and ribboned-off pews and sea of ushers in tuxedos.

"You think we'd get in trouble if we slipped out for a hamburger?" Red said now, wriggling his socked feet on Mother's porch.

I had to laugh. "Deep trouble," I said. I told him I'd been thinking about that myself, how we used to do that, back when we'd been free to go (although it hadn't seemed like freedom at the time) whenever we wanted to.

"You always got the chiliburger," he recalled.

"I could order a beer now. I'm of age."

"You could have shared mine then."

"Whoa," I said. "I was in enough trouble in those days." But I tried to imagine how that would have been, us passing that bottle back and forth, in the confines of his junky used foreign car, books and papers all over the backseat. Dangerous is how that would have been. But maybe that was a woman in her forties thinking that; the girl in her teens, that Ella, she had only Buddy on her mind.

"You helped me out a lot of times," he said.

"Same here." I let that sit a minute, feeling comfortable with him. Then I said, "I can't believe you really still eat hamburgers. I almost fell out when I saw you scarfing Daddy's best scrambled eggs in there. What happened to the big low-fat diet you were on last time we were here?"

He leaned his elbows on his knees, looking at his feet. "I guess I've sort of reverted to type, cooking for myself."

Ouch. Without meaning to, I'd brought us back to my sister. Reminded him he was running a household alone. "Sorry," I said.

"That's okay. I have to deal with it."

When my daughter's voice reached us from the living room, we smiled at one another, in relief that we could get our minds on another generation.

"So, congratulations, Borden," Birdie blared. "That's neat, you going to Yale. I mean, if you care about college and everything."

"Thanks, yeah," my older nephew responded, his voice deeper than Red's. After a pause, adding, "You in a religious group, or something?"

"Me, why?" she asked.

"I mean, how you look and all——" He cleared his throat.

"You mean my not shaving my legs? I don't have to," my daughter told him. "Anyway, nobody notices."

"Sure they do. I did. People notice everything."

"They notice you, you mean. You're going to *Yale*."

Borden sounded patient but determined. "They notice every little thing about everybody. That's what they talk about. They're asking at your school, 'Why doesn't Birdie Hopkins shave her legs?' "

She giggled.

Bailey spoke up, his voice younger, uncertain. "Gnat-brain means you could look good if you wanted to, Birdie."

Birdie sounded angry. "You mean I *don't,* is what you're saying."

"You could look like some of the girls in West Lake Hills," Bailey told her. "Where, you know, we used to live. They, ummm, fix up? Like spend a lot of time? I mean, it isn't that, ummm, jumper-thing you've got on."

"Are they big, like me?"

"You, big?" Borden laughed a grown man's laugh. "You're

a half-pint, half the size of me. You mean heavy? You're not heavy, you're just not—just not developed yet."

Birdie's voice rose fortissimo. "I got my period two years ago. I am so developed."

I shut my eyes. Mother would have to be deaf not to have heard that, even two rooms away.

Red laughed. "She's something."

Sure enough, the kitchen door opened and my daddy joined the party. "Well, now, Miss Birdie, I didn't mean to leave you alone with these hoodlums. But what can you expect? One of them named for a *cheese* and the other for an *Irish whiskey*? In my day, boys got proper Bible names. Take my brother and me, Judah and Reuben. If I'd had sons, I'd have named them Samuel and Amos, strong names. I recall I might have mentioned those very names to their mother on more than one occasion when she was carrying—" He stopped, making a croaking sound. He must have said that same thing so often he hardly heard himself anymore, but now he made a sort of moan. "Forgive an old man, boys."

Red moved his chair closer to mine. He put a hand on my arm, getting my attention, then dropped it. I thought how hard it must be for him, everyone reminding him, not meaning to, about my sister. Feeling sad about that, and still feeling close to him, relaxed, it caught me off guard when he said, "The visit with you last summer meant a lot to Terrell, Ella. She spoke of it often."

I felt the way I'd used to in his old car with him, when we'd be talking around, and then he'd ask, "Do you think she'll ever marry a mutt like me?" Reminded that the point was about *her,* not about *me.* Earlier, I'd been a wreck because I knew everybody would bring up her supposed trip to see me, and I'd have to lie again. But then I'd forgotten; my mind, naturally, on my mother from the minute I walked in the door. "Yes," I told him, in what was partly the truth, "we really talked a lot. We'd been out of touch, well, you know that. Then, when—it all happened—I was glad we'd had that time."

"She mentioned you had a very attractive place, with a garden, as I recall?"

"A garden, yes. I do. Not like Mother's used to be. Our problem there is too much rain, the opposite of here."

"She said you drove her around the area?" He took off his tie and folded it across his knee, his eyes on me.

"I did. It was—hot. Not like this, but the way it is on the Gulf Coast, like stepping outside into a shower bath. We went to Belle Vue, that's an antebellum showplace." I went over the reunion trip I'd so carefully constructed a year ago. "We—ate in a French place, on an old brick street, a favorite of mine, the—Pink Cafe."

"So she said. Wonderful seafood."

Had I said seafood? Had she embellished? Was he testing me? Shit. I closed my eyes, then changed the subject. "She told me you'd had lots and lots of people visiting, from West Texas, friends. I guess they're harder hit out there by the drought even than here. Here at least you have the lake."

"She liked company," he said. "The boys miss that, I suspect."

I started to rise, thinking I'd fetch us iced coffee. Surely Mother couldn't object to that. But then there was Birdie, come to join us.

"My boys giving you a hard time?" Red asked her, pulling up a spare chair.

"They were just doing what boys do, Uncle Rufus. Boys are competitive all the time, every minute, and when they're trying to be nice, they tell girls how they can look as good as the girls they think are cute. They can't help doing that. They don't have brains that can understand that I don't want to look like the girls in West Lake Hills where they used to live."

Red nodded. "We're like that," he admitted. "I know your aunt often wished she'd had a daughter."

"That's why I'm named Robin, because Aunt Terrell liked that name and she didn't have a girl." Birdie looked at me, pleased at herself for knowing this.

I wished, actually, at that exact moment that my mother would join us on the porch, scold us for something in her mannered way. Any interruption to prevent Red from saying what he was bound to say next.

"I bet your aunt called you 'Robin' when she came to visit you last year, didn't she?"

Birdie looked at him, then at me, as if I might be holding a cue card. "I didn't see Aunt Terrell since I was nine, did I? Mom?"

Red waited, that same patient, expectant look on his face, more lined, less tanned than I remembered.

Birdie stared at me—no doubt reading panic. Hesitant, she suggested, "Maybe I was at school?"

"In the summer?" He shook his head.

For a moment the three of us sat there, not moving, me biting my lip because my promise to Terrell had got my daughter in this bind. Then, in half-time, Birdie loosened the gray tie, letting her hair fall in waves about her shoulders. She stood, still, the way she did, composing herself, before she drew her bow across the cello. Before a performance. She gave a little laugh. "I forgot, Uncle Rufus. I forgot it was summertime. That's when I was gone on our String Project retreat. I and Felice do that every year."

Red looked at my daughter as if his ace had been trumped, but the glance was fond. He gave the slightest (so slight I might have imagined it) nod in my direction.

I let out my breath.

Birdie smiled at us and drifted back into the living room to join the boys, where my daddy was pontificating on the history of higher education. Something Birdie said earlier nagged at me. "What did Birdie mean, saying 'West Lake Hills where the boys used to live'?" I remembered my daddy saying that some changes had already been made, when I'd asked about Terrell's big house on the lake, but then Mother had put an end to that talk.

"We moved." Red laced up his shoes, rubbing an ankle. He sat up, putting his tie back on. His eyes looked tired, though he kept them on me. "I moved, and then, after the crash, they moved in with me." He reached for glasses that weren't there, then clasped his hands, leaning forward. "Actually, we're in my dad's house, out in Pflugerville. When I decided to leave the law firm, I made inquiries about buying it back." He cracked his knuckles. "I'll give you our new address."

"I don't understand, Red. You moved out?"

"It's a long story."

He stood. "Give me your address. I'll send you a copy of today's best photo."

"When did you move?"

He stood there a spell, his hazel eyes fixed on mine. "I left, thinking the boys would stay behind with her, the weekend before she died."

9

We—my parents, Birdie, and I—saw Red and his boys to the door. There wasn't a lot of talk. Mother's party was over. Borden and Bailey must have been eager to get back to their own life; Daddy looked sad to see them go. "Don't wait so long," he said, giving each grandson a vast two-armed hug. "Don't forget we need to see you."

"Sure, Granddad," both boys told him.

Red had put his navy sports coat back on and he looked again like R. Rufus Hall, attorney-at-law. He patted his shirt pocket, which held my address. I nodded, indicating I remembered I had his. He was going to send us a photo, and that would be nice, to frame one of Birdie, with a real family. I'd promised to write sometime, let him know how we were doing. Not an appealing idea: lying to someone else by mail was at the bottom of my list.

"So long, Ella," he said.

"Take care of yourself, Red," I told him.

Birdie leaned up and kissed his cheek, which he seemed to appreciate. "Can I ask you something, Uncle Rufus?"

"Shoot."

"Why does my mom call you *Red,* and everybody else calls you *Rufus?*"

"When I met your aunt and your mother, I was still going by the nickname I grew up with. But 'Red Hall' didn't seem like much of a name for a grown man."

"How come they called you that? You don't have red hair."

"My daddy named me Rufus," he explained, "after my granddad, whom he admired considerably. But my mom couldn't abide the name. He always joked she called me 'Red' after a football player she'd dated."

Birdie nodded. "I bet she didn't like it because it sounded like a black name. I have a friend, Felice Roberdeau, she plays the flute, and the teachers are always getting us mixed up. I mean, who would you think is the black kid—Felice Roberdeau or Birdie Hopkins?" She blared out a laugh.

"You could be right," he conceded. "But my mom would never have admitted to it."

"Our teachers don't either."

When they had gone, Daddy took my daughter off into the library to look at his CD collection, or she took him, maybe, and Mother and I sat together on the porch, I in one wicker chair, she in the other, on each side of the glass-topped table where she'd carefully set her half-empty china cup. She'd removed her pearls, but remained in her yellow silk dress. No mention had been made during the morning about missing church for brunch, and I wondered if she still ever went to the old downtown Episcopal church. Some young clergyman from across the lake had done the memorial service for Terrell. To my knowledge, Mother hadn't gone for years. If she had, my sister hadn't mentioned it.

"That was a thoughtful thing, Ella, to send the old-fashioned chain letter that the friend of yours found. I do recall that era—goodness, I would have been younger than Robin. That seems another life, of which I haven't thought in years. We also sent one another handkerchiefs, and, I believe, candies and valentines, and even poems." She looked amused. "Young girls."

"I thought you might have saved—"

"Not so much as a canceled stamp, dear. When I married your dad and moved here to Austin, I quite left everything else behind."

"I'd like to have seen some of your letters."

Mother gestured toward my dress. "I noticed you have a streak of some sort across the shoulders of that nice green linen. Could the dry cleaners, do you think, have been careless?"

"The sun may have faded it," I said, seeing she'd put an end to any talk of her girlhood, about which I knew so little. "I wore it outdoors to a tea at Belle Vue—"

"Yes. That's a shame."

After a silence, in which I cast about for something safe to talk about, I said, "The photographs should be wonderful. That last one, especially. Those boys are growing so fast; it'll be good to catch them at this stage."

"I'm sorry, Ella," Mother replied, picking up her fragile cup and draining it, "that you didn't see fit to join us for the picture-taking."

"What?"

"You had the opportunity to provide us with three generations. I'd thought that the point in having the young people here."

Please, please, don't let her put it this way, me refusing to be photographed. I shut my eyes, at a loss. "It was supposed to be you with the grandchildren, Mother. Daddy planned it that way."

"Judah," she said. "Your father." She blinked back tears. "He arranged this for me, yes"—her voice rose—"as if I would not notice the absence of my missing daughter."

I watched as she pinched her nose to stop the tears and took a shallow breath. She stared out at her baking, dried-out yard (where my roses lay discarded, turning to sachet in the heat). "You fixed us a lovely meal," I ventured.

"My woman does a good job with crêpes." She continued to gaze out through the glass, composing herself. "Do you let that girl of yours, Robin, play with—what does one say at her age? associate with—? I was standing right there, when she told Rufus about that friend, so uncalled for."

"Oh, Mother." I made my voice light. "The Creoles attend the best schools in Old Metairie. Felice comes from an old family; she's an accomplished musician." Actually her mother sewed for a living, but, in a city with legions of balls and costume parties, that made for success. As for old, well, to be sure, most black families in Louisiana had been around a lot longer than the rest of us.

"I must say, dear, she gets that thoughtless way of speaking before she thinks from you. Calling my grandsons, your sister's fine outstanding sons, *Barnum and Bailey*. I thought I would fall right through the very floor with embarrassment."

"Mother, that was a slip." I'd been here less than twenty-four hours and had already offended her in more ways than all the grains of sand and the distant stars. How was it possible?

My sister, I recalled, had been able to talk to my mother for half an afternoon, for most of a morning, about almost nothing, making my mother's cheeks flush with pleasure. Terrell would mention a shirt she'd seen—she didn't know, maybe the neckline was too low, on the other hand, the color matched her skirt exactly. A vase she'd bought—with a sailboat etched into the crystal, so perfect for them, still, too narrow at the top for a real spray. Yet I always offended, saying too little, caring too much, bearing gifts that did not meet her standards: the antique roses, the flimsy blue purloined hanky letter, this secondhand celadon dress.

"My heart breaks for them," Mother said at last, her voice cracking. "Out there by the lake in that beautiful home she worked so hard to create, rattling around without her."

"They're not there anymore," I protested, stopping short. "You must know that. You must know they moved. Daddy said—"

"That's a lie. How dare you come to town and tell me what's what? You have no idea what you're talking about. Rufus reclaimed his old family home, a pioneer family, for a rental property. Terrell told me so herself. I'm sure they are staying there now only as a temporary measure while they make some changes in their fine home, which anyone can understand. How can they go on with all her things just where she left them, painful reminders?" She pressed a damp fine linen handkerchief to her eyes.

"Mother, you can't believe that——? You have to know that he moved out——"

"Stop it," she commanded, slamming her cup down in the saucer so hard the heirloom china cracked in two. "*That's enough.*" She began to weep. "Go home, Ella. You should never have come back."

10

Sitting upstairs in the large double room which once had been mine, I tried to cool off in the airy space kept shady by an ancient live oak on the west and deep eaves on the east, the central air-conditioning blowing the thin yellow curtains. Still stung, heated, from Mother's outburst, I crossed my bare feet and made myself breathe in and out. If I'd been living at home, I'd have hurled the empty rose vase at the floor and slammed the door.

But I'd already done that once. Run away.

Holing up until time for Daddy to call us a cab, I chased a memory of my sister, whose presence lingered in this room. A memory of the last time I'd seen her, the last visit we'd had together, five years before.

Something she'd said which I had not heard, or, hearing, had not picked up on, not understood. Small wonder: I'd been overwhelmed by her, by this poised, beautiful, above all affluent, person she'd become. Someone I scarcely knew who called to invite me to go to the market with her, to watch her buy and spend.

I asked if I could take Robin, as we called Birdie then, but Terrell had waved the idea away. What child wanted to be dragged through produce aisles? Besides, she'd lowered her voice on the phone, she had a confession to make.

Getting in her chilled new-model Volvo, I felt somewhat like a CARE package, a good deed she was doing in the name of kinship. That she might need something from me never crossed my mind. Here she was, forty-two and looking twenty-five to my eyes, looking terrific in beige linen shorts, white linen sleeveless shirt, tan espadrilles, her hair freshly highlighted a golden blond. I felt as awkward as a teenager, scruffy in old denim shorts and a T-shirt that had seen better days (saving my one decent blue bias-cut skirt and boat-necked blouse for Mother's sixty-fifth birthday lunch). I hadn't expected to hear from Terrell; I'd just washed my hair. Was staying out of trouble and Mother's way, as now, until time to make an appearance.

Terrell told me she had weekend guests from West Texas, come to go sailing in the afternoon, staying for supper, and friends from Houston late tomorrow. This was her only free time. She thought we ought to have a minute, just the two of us. Her life too incredibly busy to believe.

She'd appeared at the door, swinging car keys to indicate she couldn't stay, bringing a glow to Mother's face. "Why, look who's here! Can't you tarry for a cup of coffee, dear? See, I've already got the good Meissen out for tomorrow. Nice things should be used, I always say."

She drove us first by a new public walking garden called Central Park, planted where once only the back grounds of the state mental hospital had been, stopping in traffic so I could admire the star-shaped bed of Texas wildflowers— yellow coreopsis, orangey-red Indian paintbrushes, cerulean bluebonnets—blooming far past their natural season. Then we parked and entered a labyrinth of cavernous connecting rooms filled with more edibles and perishables than I had ever seen: Central Market, the Louvre of food.

Feeling like a refugee, a charity case, I tagged along behind her through warehouse-size spaces heaped with pyramids of potatoes, mountains of rare mushrooms, lettuces beyond imagining, imported cheeses and butters from every corner of the earth, flavored milks thick as cream, loaves of crusty buttermilk bread, still-warm scones fragrant as perfume. Meat rooms bejeweled with filets of beef and racks of lamb. Fish rooms studded with shellfish on ice, overlapped like roof tiles.

Silent, I watched while Terrell selected her heart-healthy foods. An orange roughey from New Zealand, a yellowfin tuna from Japan, each costing more per pound than I spent for meat in a week, baby spinach, hearts of romaine, free-range chicken breasts without the skin, melons whose names I'd never heard. Pausing while the fishman packed her seafood in bags of ice, she explained that she'd got Rufus on a low-fat, low-salt diet. Lawyers, she explained, were under so much stress. They didn't watch their cholesterol. Staring at the calorie-skimping opulence, I'd tried to imagine the law student that I'd known eating such fare, the Red who'd lived on hamburgers and ice cream, who'd kept a can of salted peanuts in his packed car. His Peugeot a snack on wheels.

"I used to bring things to the folks, but they have their set ways. I don't bother anymore. Daddy is going to cook what he has a mind to. I got tired of shelling out a small mint for something, knowing it would spoil in the back of the fridge over there."

Her car packed (the most perishable items in a small ice chest), she led me to a slatted wooden deck under an air-cooled canopy and we had designer coffee and just-baked Belgian-chocolate croissants. "I love this stuff," she said, licking a bit of the bitter sweet from her manicured nail, "but I don't keep it at home."

Tongue-tied, not able to think of anything to ask her, not comfortable bringing up our early times, I watched young mothers nearby in Bermuda shorts and tennis shoes herding small children in bike shorts and muscle shirts. Everyone eating: Blue Bell Supreme Homemade Vanilla dripping at ten o'clock in the morning.

I'd tried to fit the Red I'd known, the one who'd doted on her, waited so long to marry her, into this abundant world. I remembered him hanging around, with his unruly hair and horn-rims, my daddy saying, "Here comes Clarence Darrow." My mother, not amused, replying, "I'm sure once Rufus takes the bar, such a stress for a young man, up all night studying, they have to, for those grades, he'll leave certain things behind, that little boy's nickname. . . . Such a fine young man, his family settling on all that fertile farmland when Texas was scarcely a state." And she'd been right; gradually Red had cleaned up his act. So that when I saw him at his wedding to my sister it was almost as if they'd catered him along with the food and what flowers weren't blooming in my mother's showcase late-spring garden.

The summer I'd seen him when I'd been pregnant with Birdie, fifteen years ago now, I'd hardly recognized him in the polished, urbane attorney who came in with Terrell. Yet when he walked right up to my so-obvious belly and asked me straight out, "Who's the daddy?" and I could say, which all of them must have wondered, "It's okay, it's legal," he seemed the same old Red. I'd wanted to ask him how he felt about his new establishment life. But by my next trip home when they were fighting, and by the funeral, of course, it was too late. By then, anyway, we were both in shock.

"So," Terrell had asked me, under Central Market's court-yard canopy, "what happens now, with Buddy gone? Did you ever see him anymore? How did they find you to let you know? Do you miss him?"

Surprised at her interest, that she even wondered what had happened with us, I tried to answer her as best I could. Seeing him standing, rocking back on his heels the way he always did, whether in boots or boat shoes, a big guy, blond as she was now, so good-looking it made your teeth hurt. And reliable in inverse proportion to his looks. "He called me from time to time," I recounted, gliding over my feelings about being dumped with only a marginal way to pay the rent, but more than that, being dumped when I thought we'd lit the sky with lights every time we got into bed. "To see what I was up to, if there was somebody else. He'd ask about her, 'How's the birdie?' And then I'd have to make that into a big deal for her. I guess that's the relief, that she can't feel she has a daddy anymore who doesn't want to see her. Do I miss him? Honestly, Ter, I don't know. I used to miss that guy I ran away with like crazy—and want to cut his heart out when I saw him again."

"You're lucky, you know it?" Terrell had said then, eating

the last crumb of her pastry. "You got out. No matter how mad it made Mom, you got out."

And that's what turned my head. The idea that she envied me running away, or at least had some mixed feelings on that score. I assumed that her thinking about Buddy being dead, thinking about him and me way back, had got her to missing those days. Maybe missing the way Red used to wait for her on that sunporch, the way he'd kept coming around, his staying power letting her know he was crazy about her. I wondered if maybe, in getting the elegant house and the collection of statewide friends, the prosperous husband, that she'd started missing those lovestruck, disorderly student days. Had started missing herself.

But I hadn't asked. I hadn't asked her, What was the confession you were going to make, Ter? I hadn't asked her, What's on your mind? Why did you want to talk to me today? I hadn't asked, sitting out there in the courtyard of that fancy epicurcan store that was trying to air-condition the entire outdoors, Are you happy in this swank life? I hadn't wondered. Being amazed that she, my big sister Terrell, considered *me* lucky. Lucky to have got away.

11

I spent the first week back trying to recover from the trip home. I couldn't write my mother, not one line, one word. The thick notepaper from Belle Vue lay untouched. Every time I thought of a letter, I would see my unappreciated roses left to dry, to die, attar of roses, in Mother's side yard. It was as if the rose garden of my mind had been turned to dust by the Texas heat and then battered to compost by our constant coastal rains. I said over and over, like a litany, the names of all the fine old roses Henry had selected for me to take, the roses which I had, all spring and summer, in my letters, planted, fed, watered, mulched, cut, and with which I had, in my letters as in my mind, filled vases.

The shell-pink Natchitoches Noisette with its scent of myrrh; the blush-pink cabbage rose, Fantin-Latour, "rose of painters"; the long-budded Jean Bach Sisley, delicate salmon veined in carmine; the soft yellow Céline Forestier with its odor of spice; the Souvenir de la Malmaison, once grown in the imperial gardens of St. Petersburg; the apricot Mlle. Franziska Krüger; the saucer-size Sombreuil; the Boule de Neige; Le Vésuve.

Since I'd only been gone for two days, and since, naturally, my clients were off in cooler, drier climates, I didn't feel the need to mention my absence as I set about to tend the three house gardens I'd been working on when Daddy called to invite us to the birthday weekend. The jobs were finishing, anyway; everybody homed back to Old Metairie like swallows to Capistrano when the schools opened, private schools following the public schools' schedule. I more than likely wouldn't see any of these homes again until the holidays. Or until ski season.

The wonderful courtyard with the dwarf orange and lemon trees, the white Formosa lilies and drowsy moonflowers, I might never get to water again, since the owner's decorator had a friend who tended houseplants. But the great backbreaking tubs of Ming *Aralias* and King *Segos* in the stark modern house, I'd certainly not heft again for love, though I probably would for money, given the chance.

At the Georgian home of my first and best client, I got rid of the last of the unpleasant remnants of my trip to Austin. As always, I punched in my code and set inside the six cobalt-blue jugs of purified water, let the chlorine settle out of the tap water I used on thirsty roots, pinched off fading blooms, checked the soil and light, removed here and there a yellow leaf, and said my good-byes for now to the fragrant pink and porcelain hybrids.

Then, with the baggy birthday dress over my shaky arm, I headed for the stairs. It was as if the residue of the painful visit back home, the unpleasant scene with my mother, still clung to the used green dress with the faded streak across the too-wide shoulders. I could not bear the thought of ever wearing it again, or even of having it hang, mute, a reminder, in my closet. Of course it was dumb, deciding to cast off a dress I'd spent such a great amount of time and such a modest amount of cash procuring. And worn only once. But such was my reaction to the very sight, the very presence of the oversized thrift-shop bargain.

I climbed the wide grand stairway, crossed the dark polished-oak hall, entered the bedroom with its thick white rug bordered with white cabbage roses. Taking shallow breaths (as if in the first stages of labor), I moved past the high bed with its antique-white spread on which the two rare gray Chartreux cats opened and closed their yellow eyes at me.

Trembling, I began to move the padded hangers, having this crazy notion that somehow this offending dress should be left here, in partial payment, interest due, for the coveted black dress. Color by color, I moved the linens, silks, French cottons, chiffons, until, at the back of the rack, next to the floor-to-ceiling cases for shoes, I found a bottle-green suit with a skirt clearly the wrong length for today's styles—too long to be short, too short to be long—of a stiff brocade. The perfect concealment. Slipping mine beneath it on the hanger, an undergarment for the finer garment, I quickly buttoned the thick frog fasteners across the lifeless linen chest. As I finished, still shaky, I fancied that perhaps my discarded dress had once come from this very closet and so had made its way, like a pilgrim, back where it began.

By the weekend, I had put all that, the visit, behind me. Things in the real world had returned to normal. On Saturday, I sat at the kitchen table, under the ceiling fan, trying to go over my accounts (jobs done, jobs possible) and waiting for the plumber. While we'd been in Austin, the tailend of the tropical storm had petered out up the coast in some cotton farmer's acreage, but not before leaving us with a pond-size pool in the backyard, a squishy marsh in the front, and a backed-up commode and sink in the rental half of my duplex, with my tenant, the teacher, due to return next week.

I'd called my main drain man, a youngish guy I'd persuaded a couple of years ago to drop by on the weekend after a torrential rain and bail me out. "I get overtime on weekends," he'd said. "Think of me as a job you wouldn't otherwise have," I'd countered. "Take your wife to Paris on me." "Ha, ha," he'd replied, but it had been my experience that all plumbers shared a pride in being paid like neurosurgeons for less fatal results. Now he dropped by after he tended to emergencies, when things were slow.

Karl had called midweek, in the late afternoon, getting Birdie on the phone. She had practiced doubly since we got back because of having had to miss one String Project rehearsal for the birthday brunch, but to listen to her talk to Karl about it, her trip to Texas had been *major*. She'd managed to bring back with her three CDs featuring cellos, which she played at top volume on our boom box in the front room whenever possible, morning, noon, and night, before our housemate returned to object.

Daddy had also, as we went out the front door of the yellow frame house, pressed cash into my hands to cover both taxi rides. I'd have eaten fishing worms for a month before I'd have asked him, but I didn't refuse. (Having gone into debt taking them out for the Mexican meal.) "Your mother," he'd said, making excuses for her absence when we left, "wore herself out. She's gone down for a nap. Come again, Ella. Don't wait such a spell. We're getting too long in the tooth to stretch out these reunions." And I'd promised, crossing my fingers behind my back, that we would. Except that Birdie looked so pleased, and gave him such a squeeze, and thanked him for the fortieth time, that she made me ashamed, and I uncrossed them. "Sure," I told him. "We need to see you, too."

"Auf Wiedersehen," he said, looking sad.

"Au revoir," I responded.

"Bye." Birdie had stood on tiptoe and mashed her face into his beard. "Bye. Bye."

When I'd got on the phone with Karl, he asked, "How'd the trip go? Sounds like the Bird had a ball."

"The hanky letter was the highlight," I lied. "Thanks." Then I added a bit of truth. "I missed my sister."

"I think that's what shook my dad's apples loose from his tree, losing his brother—a younger brother at that."

Karl was an only child like Birdie, and maybe that's what made his not having kids more painful. You needed somebody to share a childhood with. "How's he doing?" I asked, to let him know I knew all families had problems. "Your dad."

"He hardly moves out of his chair anymore. I try to tell Mom it's clinical, but she says he's just mule lazy." He sounded sorrowful: a German without a father. "You want to see a movie? There's this new one about some guy whose whole life appears on TV."

"Sunday maybe?"

"It's a sleeper."

"I'll buy the popcorn."

Now, hearing Birdie's voice outside, I turned on the window AC unit and unlocked the door, sticky, barefoot, not one hair of my just-washed head in place. I hadn't bothered about how I looked all week; it was as if, be it ever so humble and the rest, it was a relief, a reprieve, to be home, in my own space, nobody passing judgment. Not having to be anyone I was not.

"Mom, we're here—," my daughter said, pushing through the door, motioning behind her to Felice and Felice's mother, Mayfair.

"Sorry to barge in—," the woman said.

"Please. You were so good to have Birdie overnight." I slipped on my sandals and held out my hand, wishing I'd at least combed my hair. "Iced coffee?" I gestured to the other wooden kitchen chair.

"Definitely. The air conditioner in my van has run out of whatever they put in there. Freon? Or is that the Greek king?" She pressed the icy glass against her milk-chocolate cheek.

"I hope you're not asking me," I said.

"My dad's a preacher. He gets off to that Greek business."

"My daddy likes Old Testament names. His is Judah."

"It must be that generation. We've got a couple of tribes as well, Issachar and Zebulun. My poor uncles."

I didn't know Felice's mother well, but when the girls got into the String Project and became inseparable, we became phone friends. She was near my age, with reddish-brown plaits, a trim figure. I knew that she made ball gowns and festival costumes and that to wear a dress stitched by May-fair Roberdeau meant something. And that she, too, had no man in residence.

"How'd you get the name Mayfair?" I asked her.

She smiled and shrugged. "It was an elementary school my mama couldn't go to."

Birdie asked politely, "Would you like a peanut butter sandwich, Ms. Roberdeau?"

"Honey, no. We're out the door in one instant. Felice"— she shook a finger at her tall, skinny, pretty daughter—"do not think about putting one bite in your mouth, we are headed for the service station. Ella and I are just going to have a small chat."

I wished I had at least a fresh peach or bite of cake to offer. Instead, I nodded to show I was listening, while the girls poured orange juice and disappeared into Birdie's room.

"I surmised," Mayfair said, "it might be useful to you, in your watering business over there in the wide-avenue, deep-lot section of town, to hear about what I saw at the Old Metairie Country Club." She looked proud to have this news.

"You went there?" This question and my surprise had nothing to do with her being what was generally called *black* these days, but only with her being a part of a group called *us:* people who didn't get invited to such places.

"This very morning, hon. How it happened, which you can figure out without my telling you, was these young ladies whom I am dressing, or rather whom my staff and I are dressing, were having a luncheon party at the club and somebody got the great idea that there they were, going to be all in one place, and if we brought over their gowns—these are all in shades of pink for this particular party—they could have a fitting right there in the dressing room."

"I've driven by it." I could picture the large pink Moorish country club at the end of the wide divided live-oak-shaded street, with its four tennis courts complete with judging stand, a golf course stretching green and rolling along the bayou, a sloping lawn suggesting croquet and egg hunts. In fascination, I attended to every detail as Mayfair spoke, my mind thinking *Dear Mother, Dear Mother*, for I still had been unable to put pen to paper since my return.

. . . Some of the garden clubs arranged a luncheon in the Petit Wedgwood Room of the Old Metairie Country Club, quite a beautiful space. They'd just celebrated their seventy-fifth year, and gave us a little tour, showing off the antique thirty-six-foot French pewter bar and inlaid pewter wall panels, the refurbished men's grill, and the new wide gallery porch looking toward the bayou, with ceiling fans and everywhere the scent of potted ginger . . .

"I thought," Mayfair continued, "that the next time one of your plant women in her big house gets to talking about the Club—you get what I'm saying, Ella, the way they definitely must do, talk on and on about whatever place or event they are excluding us from—you could happen to mention you have some familiarity with the place yourself."

"Thanks," I told her. "That was a treat to hear all that, since I never expect to set foot inside the door."

"You'd know all the plants on that big porch."

"I'd like to see them—"

She rose, calling out to her daughter, "Felice, child, we have to move along."

"Come again," I said.

Sitting alone at the table, I repeated aloud, ". . . and everywhere the scent of potted ginger." But I could not pick up the pen, could not reach out for the heavy notepaper from Belle Vue. Instead, I slipped out of my sandals and waited while Birdie, changed into her baggy shorts, set out the paper plates for our lunch. Thinking I should do something with my wet hair.

When someone banged on the back door, I assumed it was the plumber. Naturally, arriving when I'd given up on him.

"Hi, Uncle Rufus," I heard Birdie say, peering out through the screen.

"Hi, yourself."

"You're supposed to say 'Guten Tag,' " she explained, letting him into where I sat paralyzed in my chair. "Would you like a peanut butter sandwich?"

12

"hanks, I would," Red said, taking off a gray seersucker jacket and hanging it on the doorknob. Seeing there were only two chairs at the small round table, he leaned against the counter, as if he were comfortable, as if his good shoes weren't filled with water from wading through our yard.

"With banana slices or bean sprouts?" Birdie asked him, into her role of luncheon hostess, seemingly not the least bit nonplussed to have this kinsman in our house.

"Banana would be great," he said, smiling at me.

For a moment I couldn't move, could hardly breathe. Of all the people in the world (save one), he was the person I least wanted to have show up at my back door. I'd painted myself—at those careful Texas birthday-party reunions—as someone I was not, living in a gracious world which did not exist. I felt my face turn red with shame. The shame of having been found out.

Deciding I'd never looked more a mess in my life, I went into the front room and brought him a straight chair. We only used the small living room to listen to music, or, sometimes in the evening, by myself, I'd sit in there in the dark when it was cool and listen for the train to come by at eleven, and think about how things had worked out.

"Here," I said to Red, "sit." I put out flatware and a paper plate, and handed him a glass of iced coffee, finishing off the jar I kept in the fridge. I also handed him a towel to dry his feet.

"I'm sorry, Ella," he said. "I intended to call first, but I had a map from Hertz and I could see it was going to be easier to find the street than to locate a pay phone."

"You caught us in." I shrugged. What difference would it have made, anyway, if he had called ahead? I'd have told him we had strep throat or weekend plans, that he had the wrong number. No way would I have let him come here, if I'd had a say. Good thing Birdie (trusting, friendly Birdie), who now served us our sandwiches, had gone to the door.

"Ella—" He seemed about to make some sort of explanation.

Ever so slightly, I shook my head.

"Uncle Rufus—" Birdie made table conversation with our guest. "I'm going to meet my friend Felice at the Pink Mall this afternoon. That's not far and Mom lets me walk."

"I want to take your mom out to dinner. Is that going to be a problem?"

"She's probably going to the movies with Karl," she said, her eyes cutting to me. "That's what my mom sometimes does on Saturday night."

I smiled her a thank-you. "We'll work it out. I'll see if Felice can come back here with you later. You two are big enough to stay here by yourselves, if you keep the door locked."

As could have been predicted, the plumber took that minute to rap on the door, and I had to take him around the front to the rental half of my duplex, leaving Red alone with my child. "Why don't you take your uncle into the living room?" I suggested to her. "I won't be long." We had a decent two-person sofa in our crowded front room, two stuffed chairs, all covered in the now-faded Picasso blue that once was my favorite color, and a small woven rug of mixed blues, made in the low country of Louisiana. No plants, though. I didn't want to have to look after them at home as well. Instead, I read my stack of catalogues: antique roses, Southern gardens, Old Metairie garden tours.

"Would you like to see my cello?" Birdie asked him. "I mean the cello I get to use?"

In the other half of the house, the plumber flipped the pages of his metal-backed ledger. "You called this same time last year," he remarked. "You might think about getting the Roto-Rooter guys in, maybe think new pipes."

"I'm not thinking about anything but having this place so the john flushes and the tub empties and the sink drains before the teacher gets back from summer in Virginia with her folks."

"I understand," he said. Understanding that we were talking about money. "That your family I saw in there?"

"That's them."

"Nice. I got me two girls."

"I'm glad, Bert." I left him to do his job and made a call out on Margot-the-teacher's line. Explaining to Mayfair that my brother-in-law had blown in, catching me in disrepair,

and asking could she lend me Felice to stay here with Birdie
for a while in the late afternoon and evening, so I could
show him the sights. Birdie had the house key on a ribbon
around her neck, I told her. I also asked what she knew
about the Pink Cafe, where I knew I was going to have to
take him.

"Try the crab cakes," she said with authority. "Ask the
waiter if he'll tell Daniel—that's the chef—you'd like the
corn galettes. They're never on the menu, but he usually has
some. Suggest to the guy that you two split the tarte tatin
for dessert—"

"Maybe *you* should take him—?" I joked weakly.

"Show him the Old Metairie Country Club. Mention the
French pewter inlays."

"Sure. He'll believe that. Me, coming from this place,
pretending I know that place."

"Hon, you have to think like a man. You're staying in that
small gem of yours because the price of land in that area is
skyrocketing. Tell him they'll buy it for a teardown, you'll
get a quarter mil for the lot."

Hanging up, I banged my head softly against the rental
bedroom wall. I might as well be back at Mother's house
putting on a show, lying my head off.

When I got back, the plumber bribed and thanked, Birdie
was explaining to Red all about the String Project, and how
they provided the instruments, and how you tried out. Presenting her life in her forthright, truthful way—and, of
course, unwittingly presenting a wealth of other information. Seeing me come through the doorway, she mentioned

the apocryphal annual String Project retreat, intuiting that this surprise visit was not entirely pleasing to her mom. (And because her heart was made of gold.)

What, I wondered, joining them, sinking into the other cushion of the sofa beside Birdie, would my sister Terrell want me to do now that Red was here? Carry through with the charade? Describe her visit here, what we did, what we talked about? But surely, having waded around to my back door (the notice on the front said BELL DOESN'T WORK, GO AROUND BACK), and sized up me and this run-down two-plex, he must have known at once that he'd found something different from what he'd made this trip expecting.

I told Birdie that Felice could come back with her from the Pink Mall, that I'd leave them spaghetti, that Red and I were going to drive around, then have an early supper.

"I and Felice can fix something, Mom."

"You go on. And be careful."

"I'll see you later, Uncle Rufus. Won't I?" She threw her arms around him.

"Sure thing," he promised. "So long."

"Au revoir," she replied.

Alone with Red, I felt both relieved and nervous. Relieved, because I wouldn't have my daughter hearing whatever I chose to tell him. Nervous, because I was going to have to make believable my sister's visit. It seemed to me his coming here was akin to someone paying for a ticket, taking a seat, watching the curtain rise, expecting to see a performance of *A Tale of Two Sisters,* and instead, seeing only the backstage crew checking the lights, the extras picking

up their props, the stars getting made up, wardrobe un-
packing the costumes. My task, as I saw it now, taking a
deep breath, was to make Red think the production—Terrell's visit to my supposedly genteel surroundings—had all
been crafted by my sister and me to fool our mother. Not to
deceive him.

"So, what's the agenda here?" I asked him straight out.

"I want to see where you took Terrell. I came on impulse.
If that's difficult for you, to be reminded—"

"I'll be about fifteen minutes," I told him, heading into
the kitchen's tiny work space, turning on the burner, chop-
ping up onion, fresh tomatoes, a garlic clove, until I covered
the bottom of a hot skillet, adding a little oil, ground meat,
then putting it on low. While this simmered down to a
sauce, and the water boiled for pasta, I went into my bedroom, behind the table where Red sat waiting in his sock
feet.

Well, now, I silently addressed my open closet, what have
you got to offer? My best watering shorts, but maybe the
Pink Cafe expected something a bit dressy. Besides, he'd
worn a jacket. I pulled on a black T-shirt and, on top,
donned an oldish café au lait sleeveless dress, leaving it
unbuttoned to the waist. Good? Awful? My brown sandals
were already on my feet, matching well my now partially
dry hair, which I tried, with little success, to fold into a
French braid by myself. Giving up, I held it back on each
side with semi-new tortoise barrettes. A nice sienna lipstick
completed the look: ready for Red.

The boiling water had raised the humidity in the kitchen
to 89 percent, cooking in minutes the dry lengths of

spaghetti, which, drained, I left on the counter with a note explaining how to resuscitate it (plunge into boiling water) and that the sauce was in the fridge to be heated. They could add Birdie's seven-grain bread to fill up.

"Okay," I said to Red, feeling as ready as I'd ever be. I showed him the drill for navigating hurricane aftermath on the Gulf Coast. You carry your socks and shoes. I didn't say that nobody down here wore socks, since he had lace-up shoes, but maybe next time, if there was a next time (I guess I was thinking about that), he'd know to wear boat shoes or sandals. In the driveway, shaking my feet off like a dog just out of the lake, I told him, "We'll leave your rental car and go in mine. These streets are a maze of the worst kind; visitors sometimes are lost for several months. I'm surprised you found us."

"I spotted your street right off the access road."

"I'd have met your plane."

"I was afraid you wouldn't."

"A fifty-fifty chance I would have." I laughed and cleared a place for him to sit in my heirloom Chevy, moving a notepad, a pair of old tennies, garden gloves, and an empty water bottle to the floor of the backseat. "Does this remind you of your old car?"

"I hated selling it, the worst way."

"What'd you get for it?" I backed carefully out the drive to the sloshy, unpaved road.

"I forget. Forty-five cents on a new Peugeot? Fifty-five?"

I turned to look at him, glad to have him in my car. He wore wire-rim glasses, which he hadn't had at Mother's, though maybe he wore his contacts for her benefit. He looked more like himself, even in the high-fashion Oliver People's frames. Getting into this car, shutting the doors, heading out, did remind me of our old drive-up hamburger days. It was intimate to be alone with a man in a car, it was. You could hear him start to speak, hear him shift in his seat, cough, sense his shoulder close by. And nobody could hear what you said to one another and nobody could see how you looked at one another.

I got a grip on myself and began the tour. "The railroad track there," I explained, "is the south dividing line of Old Metairie, and therefore of the school district, which is the reason we're camped out here."

"Good location." He turned half facing me, his seat belt loosened, half looking out the window. He seemed fairly at ease, considering how men hated being a passenger in a car. He tossed his jacket in the backseat while my AC struggled to come to life.

"I owe our place, such as it is, to Buddy."

"I never understood what you saw in that big handsome guy with all the macho moves."

"You mean you never understood what he saw in me. I got him on the rebound."

"That wasn't what I meant."

I turned around and drove us back through the sheltered enclave of pastel homes that formed Old Metairie—going fifteen miles an hour on the dogleg streets that zigged and zagged so that outsiders couldn't cut through the pricey area, or find their way anywhere unless they already knew how to get there. Even here, in the high-maintenance neighborhoods, you could see some storm damage: soggy yards, flattened caladium, a sagging crape myrtle, a broken althaea branch. I pointed out to Red a narrow blue-painted home, a frame house one room wide, with porches top and bottom. "You see these shotguns in Central Texas. The old German settlers built them, as they did here." And then slowed before a lavender story-and-a-half with dormers, porch swing, mulberry shutters. "This is called a cottage here, modeled, as a lot of them were, after small English country places. The French really settled the adjoining parish, not here." I pulled up at the curb of a familiar Dutch-pink house with white picket fence and white shutters, shaded by a tall magnolia, past its bloom. "I gave Terrell a photo of this house," I said carefully, "to show our mother." I hesitated, the car idling.

But Red did not comment. He did not say: You pretended you lived in that house. He did not say: My wife pretended to me she had stayed in that house. He looked at me, and we sat there for a time, until I moved on.

By now I'd relaxed considerably. I'd become so used to writing Mother about these streets, these very houses and yards as if they were on my street, as if this neighborhood was mine, that it all seemed natural. Crawling along, making the leisurely turns, I found it so completely plausible that Terrell and I had indeed scouted about to find things to photograph for Mother, to relate to Mother, that I myself almost believed we'd done it. My sister, with her golden hair, in her beige linen shorts and white sleeveless linen blouse, asking could we stop someplace for coffee and a pastry.

"At her memorial service," Red spoke aloud from his own private thoughts, "you said, 'I'm glad you're still standing.' That was the most real thing anybody said to me, Ella. I wanted to thank you for that."

"It seemed to me that losing someone that way, the way you did, when you were in the midst of"—I hesitated, wanting to say it right—"unfinished business, would nearly lay you out flat as an asphalt drive."

"That's about the size of it," he admitted, wiping his wire-rim glasses.

"You sure were a help to me when I came back home pregnant, and everybody else pretended not to notice."

"I thought maybe I'd stepped out of line, mentioning it."

"You probably had. I'd stepped out of line even showing up. But I wanted to flaunt my belly, however they took it. I owe that to Buddy, too."

He put his hand lightly on my shoulder. "You got a good girl out of it."

Working my way through the maze of short streets, turning left, right, left, right, I waved an arm at the small lots with their rectangles of grass, front beds edged in monkey grass, wisteria growing along the eaves. "Once these were places where my plumber, Bert, could have lived, or Margot, the teacher who rents half my house, or our mail carrier."

"Or my folks."

"Or your folks. Now these go for three times the price of my parents' house."

"How come?"

"Safety. One lock on the door, only decorative fences in the yards. You can take a walk in the evenings. Kids can shoot baskets in the driveways. Fifties' safety at nineties' prices, my friend Karl says. He's a realtor."

"The one Birdie mentioned." He smiled.

"Protecting her mom." I smiled too.

I drove him out of the area and then back between two stone pillars into the hidden heart of *old* Old Metairie, with its walled gardens, gated drives, historic houses, private police force. Cruising down one of the wide divided streets, ancient live oaks meeting above our heads, I felt on familiar ground. "This is where most of my clients live," I told him.

"Your clients?" He sounded surprised.

I'd forgotten that he had no inkling of what I did. But why should he? To my mother, and my daddy, too, even to my sister, a good marriage, or even a good widowhood, for that matter, meant the woman did not have to work. "I water houseplants," I explained. "I'm a plant sitter, like a house sitter or a pet sitter." And, from where we were, I could see the rose lady's Georgian home, and knew, two streets over, exactly where moonflowers dozed next to Formosa lilies and how the daylight would look filtered through the skylight.

At the end of the street, I lingered before the pink Moroccan flat-roofed facade of the country club. Six tennis courts lay under wet tarps beside a reviewing stand covered in see-through plastic. A temporary awning sheltered arrivals at the front door. But I did not pretend to know about the new gallery porch along the back with its scent of potted ginger, the Petit Wedgwood Room, or even the famous inlaid pewter bar brought from France. Then I turned and slowly drove back up the street we'd just come down, out of the secure, secluded compound.

"Did she—" Red looked out the window at the homes, rubbed the back of his neck, then clasped his hands. "That must be interesting work," he finally said.

"Yes," I agreed. "I love flowers."

13

I decided to take Red to Belle Vue next. A place that was real, that I loved, and where I supposedly had taken Terrell. I wanted him to see where the roses I stuffed beneath the rudbeckia at Mother's came from, and maybe understand how it hurt to bury them there. But when I pulled into the gravel drive and cut the ignition, my mind stayed on my sister, and for a moment I felt that loss and wondered what I was doing taking Red around, playacting our sisterly visit, when maybe now it didn't matter. But I'd made her a promise; I was keeping my word. Besides, if she *had* come (and in my mind I'd begun to think *when* she had come), I would certainly have brought her here to meet Henry, and to see his flowers.

After paying the nominal admissions fee to tour the house and grounds, I led Red past the long reflecting pool enclosed by a boxwood hedge, the lily-pad pond with one hundred kinds of ferns on the banks, the English-countryside garden with its stone benches, longstemmed grasses, trumpet vines, and bleeding hearts, to an extended trellis with a dozen different climbing roses.

"I started coming here to learn from Henry, the head gardener, but then I began to write to Mother about my favorites, pretending they were growing in my own garden." I laughed, embarrassed to reveal the depth of my deception. "But you saw my yard—"

"Did Terrell—" But he let that go. He'd left his jacket in the car and rolled up his white shirtsleeves. The humidity had wilted him a bit, and, perhaps, the strain. He looked less like a lawyer than what Daddy used to call, speaking of his studious junior colleagues, a pencil pusher. He clipped sunglasses on his wire-rims and looked around. "This must have been some estate in its day."

"This is still its day."

We found Henry stooping over, his knees muddy, his face shaded under a wide-brimmed straw hat. He didn't hear us till I called his name, then with some difficulty he rose and wiped his hands to shake mine.

"Thank you," I told him. "The rose bouquet looked beautiful. Each and every one survived the trip and kept its fragrance all weekend."

He looked pleased. "Your mama liked our selection, then, did she?"

"She almost cried," I lied. "Texas has been so hot, her own garden has dried to straw."

He lifted his large hands to the sky. "We drown; they scorch." He seemed to consider this the natural way of things.

I introduced the men. "This is Rufus Hall; he's family. Red, this is Henri Legrand; he's my teacher."

"Don't know about that, Ella," Henry said, but he reddened a bit under his sun-browned skin. He did at that moment, straw hat under his arm, face lined as worn leather, look like a farmer in the Rhône Valley. Or so I imagined. He showed Red his new prize from West Sussex, England, bred in Hamburg when that was part of Denmark, an Alba out of a Damask. He could have been reciting the lineage of queens and emperors, instead of a hybrid of near-perfection, deep-to-palest pink, which could flourish anywhere—except at my mother's house.

"How long have you been working here?" Red asked, sounding deferential. He seemed to study the older man with something akin to envy.

Henry shifted his weight, taking Red's measure. Was this a genuine question? "I was gardener here when it was a private home. They let me stay on. Now they've got a dozen working, and I'm called Head Rose Gardener. That suits me fine. I always did favor the roses."

"Ella must have got that from you."

"Might be," he agreed, putting his straw hat on, getting down on his knees. Back at work. He indicated the troughs he was shaping around the base of the rosebushes. "I'm trying to drain their roots."

"Glad to meet you," Red said, standing a minute, as if to add something more.

He and I walked along to a wooden bench under a lattice laced with white clematis, rooted in a limey soil. I sat, kicking off my sandals and pulling up the skirt of my dress enough to get hazy sun on my shins. I lifted my hair to try to catch a little breeze on my neck, but the sticky air hung still.

Red, beside me, stretched out his long legs, seeming to consider them, his khaki pants still damp at the cuffs from wading through my backyard. He stared out toward the boxwood wall.

I waited. I knew he was working around to something; the way he'd rolled up his sleeves; the way he'd been distracted. Maybe he intended to get around to pinning me down; maybe he'd ask a few more of those leading questions, the way he had in Austin. I realized I was on my guard.

He cracked his knuckles, then turned, facing me. "I lost her," he said, "and it's hard to say when."

I tried to loosen my tight shoulders. I mopped my neck with a Kleenex. "How's that?" I ventured, cautious.

He studied my face as he spoke, stopping to see if he was getting through. "I spent all those years working downtown at that firm, making the kind of name or money or both that allowed the kind of life Terrell expected. Then, I don't know, one day I faced up to the fact I wasn't working for myself anymore, and not for her and my boys either. I was plain flat-out working for Agatha. I guess I figured when I got Terrell to leave that house and marry me, I'd won. But I hadn't."

I didn't know what to answer. It gave me a knot in my stomach to think that he'd gone through that, too. To think what it must have been like for him to have impersonated an attorney-at-law down to the tailored suit and rolled leather belt all those years, almost a quarter of a century, trying to be what they expected. It was as if I'd stayed in Texas, having to show up every afternoon in some borrowed, stolen, begged linen dress, my hair properly kempt, my temperament also. I wanted to say to him: My God, how did you do it? "Yes," I said, and wished I could let him know I understood the way they tried to keep you all your life the person they wanted you to be.

He took off his glasses and cleaned them. "I told Terrell I had quit the firm. I walked in to where she sat, working out the menu for another sailing weekend supper, and told her. I told my sons. Borden was in his room, trying to polish up an essay that would get him into Yale; Bailey was in his, cramming for his Kaplan SAT course. I told them all. I said, I'm picking up the pieces where I left off. I'm setting up my own practice in my old man's house. You can stay here, I told them, keep all this." He looked at me, stricken, his hands flat on his knees as if holding himself in place. "I never dreamed that the boys would end up there, with me, and hating the place." He sat silent so long I thought maybe I was supposed to comment. But then he went on, in a low voice. "She turned her back on me in bed. She said she'd kill herself before she'd tell her mother I was moving out and going to live with the cedar-choppers north of town." He rubbed his eyes with his knuckles. "I have to ask myself: did she?"

I put my hand on his arm. "No," I said. "No. Everybody feels guilty when someone dies." Hadn't I reproached myself again and again for not talking my sister out of that West Texas trip? Not telling her to wait.

"My boys won't get over it," he said.

"Let's walk around," I suggested, pulling down my skirt, wriggling into my sandals and getting up. "Henry says they've received a large donation for a hummingbird garden. I'd like to see the area. Besides, it's a bit cooler when you move around."

"How did you feel when Buddy died?"

"That's too complicated." I shook my head. How could I talk about that? "We lived apart longer than we lived together. He never knew his daughter, not really. It's not the same."

"Unresolved?" He took my arm, as if to help me down the path to the lily-pad pond, but more, I suspected, to keep me from turning away.

"Yes, of course. How can losing someone be otherwise?" But, as he sensed, I didn't want to deal with the subject any-more.

"This place have a bathroom?" He looked toward the main house.

"Inside. And a gift shop where I need to buy a box of notepaper. Let's clean up a bit here, and then I'll show you our boundary waters, and the stone church I wrote Mother about."

Back in the car, out of the air that felt damp enough to wring out, out of the steamy afternoon sun, I gave a mean-dering tour of our big muddy Mississippi and of Lake Pontchartrain, with pools of water in between. I wasn't truthin', as they said here, but I wasn't lying either: Terrell might have had this same tour. Between the two high levees that held back the tons of water, it was easy to get a sense of our below-sea-level lowlands, and to feel how temporary and chancy it was to set up residence here.

"I'd like to tell you what I'm doing," Red said, after I'd run out of commentary.

"Do," I kept hearing a phoebe sing its name over and over.

"That's what made the rift, not so much the decision to give up my partnership, but to do full time what she thought I could do pro bono. If I had to get it out of my sys-tem, as she put it."

I remembered Terrell saying that Rufus had gone strange, that he'd had a midlife crisis.

"When we were in high school, a bunch of us, kids who thought ourselves activists, went to meet the army of Valley Citrus Workers who walked all the way from the fruit orchards down there in Hidalgo, Cameron, and Willacy Counties—down at the tip of the state—to Austin to petition the governor for better working conditions. Nothing happened, naturally. They got met on the outskirts of town and sent back on their way, to walk the three hundred miles home. We got outraged, drew up petitions. We were going to do something about the workers. Then, you know the way it went, the war came. Nam gave us something worse to protest. Then, after law school, well, their march, and I guess everything we'd said we were going to do, came to seem like all the rest that had gone on in those days— history."

I nodded, moved to get this glimpse of him, young, a high school boy, a law student, in a different way.

"When the killer freeze of 1989 crippled the fruit trees and knocked us out of being one of the top three citrus states in the country, I followed it daily, the thousands out of work, the orchards closed, nobody getting hired back. I wanted to stop what I was working on then, those dozens of ways of keeping and passing on money, and do something. But—" A low sound came from his middle, as if he'd been holding his breath. "By then, my boys were going off to camp. Terrell and I had"—he seemed to choke—"taken up sailing."

"I remember the freeze—," I said.

"You do? Nobody else paid the least attention. All I got was griping because the price of orange juice had gone up."

"Well, but by then I was working to keep a roof over my head, and my small daughter's head, tending plants. My heart broke for those fruit pickers. If you made a living growing things, you were totally at the mercy of whatever water, sunlight, and weather came along. I read every scrap about that freeze, the ice-coated limbs breaking off when the sun hit, trees dying every night. I still feel it here"—I pressed my chest—"every time some gusty rain upgrades to a tropical storm and upends itself on some cotton field or rice paddy or small truck garden."

By this time I'd pulled into the parking lot of the immense old Episcopal church that was a stone-by-stone copy of St. Bartolph's in Cambridge, where I'd claimed Terrell and I had taken early communion. I was finding it hard to talk about all this while watching for stop signs and fallen branches.

Red rolled down the passenger window, as if to get some air, although the air-conditioning had kicked in with a dry, chilled breeze. "The catalyst, you could say, was a little item I saw in the paper, about a year ago. Somebody with tech money—more than likely Dell, but it didn't say so—wanted to provide citrus workers with computers. To enable not just the growers, the owners, but the pickers and packers to trade information with their counterparts in the U.S.—California, Florida—and also in Brazil, China, Spain, and Mexico. They needed a lawyer. I kept reading the thing, just an item. I carried it around. I slept on it; I wrestled with it. I tracked them down, and within a week I'd made up my mind."

I tried to get my head around Terrell receiving this news. Rufus deciding to work for citrus farmers. Rufus quitting his gilt-edged firm. I tried to even imagine her, getting in her car, crossing the low-water bridge from West Lake Hills, gunning up the hill to the yellow frame house, to tell our mother the news. "You have to understand," I said, turning to Red.

"I think I do." He leaned against the door, the window rolled back up.

"You don't," I insisted, nearly in tears at how my sister must have felt. "Look at me," I told him. "I'm on the outs with Mother; I don't see her but twice a decade. But for Terrell's funeral, at the idea of showing up there for that, even though I knew Mother would be wild with grief, I *stole a dress*." I couldn't believe I was telling him this. I hadn't told anyone, not even Birdie, who never asked about or even mentioned that black dress. "I did. I walked up the stairs of my favorite client's house and *I took a dress out of her closet*." I could feel my face grow hot. "Don't you see, Red? If I did that, so as not to upset Mother at a time like that, don't you see that Terrell just couldn't tell her about you? She just *couldn't*."

Red sat staring at me, his face blank. For the longest time he didn't speak. Then, unexpectedly, he laughed. "You sure fooled me, all right," he said. "I remember thinking, at the service, that you didn't look like the kid sister I remembered. You looked exactly like the rest of them."

I laughed, too, in relief. "I did a pretty good job, didn't I?"

14

My dinner reservation got us a small table in the back corner of the intimate, clearly costly, cafe, done in shades of pink from cameo to salmon, a single tea rose on each white cloth. I hadn't been out on a real dinner date since Karl sold two houses back-to-back, and despite the serious things Red and I had talked about, or maybe because of them, I felt more than a bit giddy to be there at the Pink Cafe, which I had more or less come to believe I'd invented. But here it was, real, candlelit, and here I was as well. I let out my breath and smiled at Red.

"This dinner's mine," he said. "I invited you."

"Thanks," I told him, then looked up, as we now had a waiter.

We got a drink, a real drink. Red ordered Scotch on ice, and I, trying to even recall what was out there besides cheap white wine by the glass, ordered a gin and tonic. We considered the menu, where, sure enough, they featured the crab cakes Mayfair had suggested. Also fresh tuna. Also sole and grouper. Just as Terrell had told him: delicious seafood. I chose the chicken with lemon-caper sauce, my mouth actually watering as I read about it.

"What do you recommend?" Red asked, the question hanging in the air between us.

I looked up, meeting his eyes. "I don't know," I said. "I haven't been here before." And, as I spoke, I knew I'd already decided to tell him the truth.

He let his shoulders sag in relief. "Thank you, Ella."

Meeting his eyes, I asked, "What do you want from me?"

He didn't hesitate. "His name."

Of course. The lover's name. All this had been about that. About the other man. I felt betrayed, though that was foolish. But I did. Felt the way you do in junior high when some guy is hanging out with you, waiting for you between classes, happening to be on his bike in your neighborhood. And then he finally asks you if you think your best friend would go out with him. Felt the way I used to, in Red's scruffy Peugeot when we'd just started chewing on our hamburgers, at that ratty drive-in by the campus, and he'd ask me: Do you think she'll ever marry a mutt like me?

Somehow, in the course of the long afternoon, I'd talked and listened to a lot of stuff, and now I'd thought, I really had, that we were having dinner because we'd done a lot of working through of our somewhat common family, and this was our reward: a cozy table for two, a good strong drink (the gin burned a pleasant path down my throat), a nice dinner to follow, then some rich dessert—with pastry, fruit, a special sauce. Something that, in my world, was scarcer than dry weather on the coast. And we could linger. After all, we were paying for the chairs. We could let the candle burn down, let its smoke mingle with the odor of tea roses.

But no. With the bird-dog personality of the true lawyer,

R. Rufus Hall must have been working toward this request since the moment he waded to my back door. Giving in to anger, not thinking of the consequences, I flared up, "Why? So you can cut his nuts off?" Being crude, realizing too late that I had trapped myself. And Terrell.

Red flushed. "Help me out here, Ella. Put yourself in my place; no, put yourself in his place."

"In his place, I'd change my name and leave the state." I ran my hand over the heavy white tablecloth, as if patting it. Across the crowded room, happier couples leaned together, hands touching by their butter plates. Damn. Damn me for being lulled.

"Someone must've contacted you when Buddy died."

"You think the guy doesn't know? Of course he knows. She was on her way out there to meet him." But I was only getting into it deeper.

"I'm sure he knows. It was in all the papers," Red agreed. "Those small airplane crashes make the news; chartered planes are the main mode of travel in West Texas."

"He could even have come to the funeral. If closure is what you're thinking about."

"He could have. The church was packed." He faltered, then continued. "She had a great many friends."

"She did. More people than I've spoken to in my entire life. Let's leave it, Red. Say the guy came to the service. Say he's dealing with it the same way we are: as best he can."

We stopped and thanked the waiter for my lemon-caper chicken and Red's fresh tuna, both savory and tender. We poked around at the food with our forks.

After I'd calmed down, I asked, "Why'd you go through

the charade of taking me to dinner, why'd you do the garden show, the boundary-water tour, if you knew about him?"

He drained his drink and signaled for another. "I didn't plan it this way, believe me. I suppose I hoped I was wrong, that I'd find she *had* been here."

"You knew better when you drove into my driveway."

He raised his hazel eyes to mine. "Tell me about him."

"Are you nuts?" I wanted to scream it at him. I could feel very wet tears leaking at the corners of my eyes. How had I got myself into this? "Look," I bargained, "let me eat my nice chicken dinner—" I wiped my face with the heavy napkin. "Let me spend a lot of time deciding which rich French dessert I'm going to eat. This isn't a daily thing in my life, Rufus."

"Tell me his name."

"I don't *know* his name."

"She had to have told you something, for you to provide her with an alibi—"

Alibi. Such a lawyer word. "Give me some time," I said.

Red called the waiter over and told him that we'd like coffee and to see the dessert menu. I considered everything. The chocolate-covered profiteroles, the caramelized tarte tatin (Mayfair's choice), the almond crème brûlée. Settling on the pear tart with crème anglaise. Red selected the flourless hazelnut chocolate cake. Neither of us considered the raspberry, apricot, or guava sorbets.

We ate our sweets slowly; we drank our hot, strong coffee. We talked about our children.

"How will it be for Borden," I asked, "going off next year?"

"He isn't bothered, though I would have been, at that age, much as I thought I wanted out of my folks' house. I guess Bailey's the one to worry about, suddenly stuck with just his dad."

"Maybe that's why I ran off first—I can't even imagine being the one kid left at home."

"Your daughter," he said, "is certainly serious about her cello."

"She loves it."

Red paid the bill; I thanked him.

When we got outside at the car, I broke down and wept, leaning my head against the driver's door, unable even to open it. "I betrayed my sister," I sobbed. "I broke my word." I could hardly see, and might have stood there all night, but the sky opened up and it began to pour.

Behind the wheel, I got myself together, put on lipstick. Red slipped out of his damp jacket and shook it. "Don't think of it that way," he pleaded. "Don't, Ella, please. I don't wish the guy any harm, can you understand that? I got to thinking, after the crash, after I could think straight enough to wonder why she'd chartered a small plane, why she'd gone out in that weather. I made a call; the Odessa Chamber knew nothing of a furniture mart, Mexican or otherwise. There had to be somebody she was meeting. That's all that made sense. It fit. Then, after I got a grasp on that, I thought, what hell, to lose someone and have to go on about your business. You and I, we had a right to grieve. Don't you see?"

I took out the barrettes and let my soaked hair loose.

"This is what I know," I said at last, worn out with it. "This is all I know. Don't ask me for any more. She called him . . .

Mr. Emu." My voice shook and I swallowed twice. "His . . .
daddy grew beef and farmed emus out in Ector County.
That's where our daddy is from. He came from a town
called . . . Notrees." I bit my lip, trying to see his expression
in the dim light. "It began—last summer."

Red leaned back against the seat. His eyes were closed.
He made a sound in his throat. "His name is Skip Rowland,"
he said. "He's a rancher. They sail on our lake." He gave the
facts in a flat voice, as if working to keep control. "I didn't—
have that figured."

For a minute, I felt really sorry for him. I knew how that
was. Even if, as he had, you've decided to move out on her,
or, as I did, you've decided to kick the guy out, neverthe-
less, there is always something in the nature of their choice
of someone who isn't you that drives a knife straight to the
heart. It's as if—the nature of what has gone wrong
between you—they need to select that which you don't
possess, have rejected, no longer set store by, and say: This is
what I most want. I'd seen it time and again. A woman
thinks she can handle it if her husband wants to run off with
a bubblehead bimbo half his age, and instead he picks an
older woman with a doctorate in a field the wife long ago
abandoned. Or a man puts all his energy into making money
and buying designer toys and his wife runs off with some kid
playing unplugged guitar, the very same instrument her
husband sold to buy his first suit. This Mr. Emu, the rancher
named Skip, must somehow be the very sort of person that
Red had least expected, and could least bear.

"Let's get out of here before we wash away," I said, pulling the car out onto the old brick street that ran behind the Pink Mall, heading us home.

Listening to the slap of the windshield wipers, I kept hearing Terrell. Remembering her saying: I'm out of my mind over him. We're head-over-heels. He wants me to leave. He wants us to get together. He wants to tell everybody. Then I could see him, her man, in my mind's eye—out there in that godforsaken dry countryside where they'd had to put down first the cattle and then the emus, baked and parched right out of business—waiting for her plane to come in. Him thinking of her out of her clothes; thinking that they were finally going to get together. I kept seeing him standing there, looking at the sky as sleet began to ice up the runway, the moisture too little and too late to help, enough only to turn the ground and the air treacherous. Skip Rowland. It did make a difference to know he had a name.

When I pulled into my driveway, I could see the kitchen light on, and the backyard light, and knew the girls were all right. I'd be glad, in truth, when the teacher was back in residence in her side of the duplex. She didn't sit, but it would be someone on the premises. I said to Red, "We'll have to take Felice home." Thinking that I owed Mayfair one for her help, even though, in the end, I'd been unable to lie about my sister's visit.

"Sure," Red said, his voice raw.

I cut off the ignition, but didn't move. "Red? Did you mean it when you said to put ourselves in his place, the guy?"

"I've been trying."

I turned so I could see his face by the yard light, the rain steady on the car roof above us. "All right, then." I took a deep breath. "We can't leave him standing out there at the end of that West Texas runway forever. I'll call him for you."

"Call him for *her,*" he said.

Then he walked around, getting drenched, and, throwing his seersucker jacket over my head and shoulders, while the two girls stood in the doorway staring, carried me across the sodden, puddled backyard into the house.

15

I felt restless, edgy, bereft in some way, after the departure of the old friend I'd been so appalled to see at my back door. I knew I'd have to write my mother, to say that Red had come, since all our children knew. But I hadn't the heart for it. A casual way to talk about what hadn't been a casual visit escaped me. And dissembling had already got me in enough of a fix.

Instead, wanting company, I called Karl on his car phone, to see if he had time, between the showing of homes in the waxing and waning neighborhoods of our bend in the coast, to spend some of it in my bed. It took a day or so until we found a few hours with Birdie gone, and all his prospective buyers taken around to homes dry enough to show. Until we had a few hours free to close my bedroom door, and, discarding our clothes on the bare wood floor, fall together for a little mutual warmth on my navy blue sheets. It wasn't great romance, or even especially steamy sex, but there was something good to be said for the feel of a friendly body, for being satisfied and satisfying.

Lying bare, cool beneath the fan, my arm across Karl's shoulders, I wondered if all German necks were flushed after the act, if all Germans dozed.

"You ever think about another kid?" he asked after a spell, rolling over on his back.

"That I got one was an outsized piece of luck."

"You could have two."

"I'm forty-three—"

"—If you had a bigger place?"

"Come on, Karl." Sometimes he got to talking about how if his wife had quit chasing around and let herself get knocked up, he could be a Sunday daddy like half the rest of the parish. I never knew what revived his regret; more than likely it was prospects looking for four bedrooms, two baths. For nurseries upstairs.

"You could start over," he said. "Have one around when the Bird starts college."

"You could find a nice young single mom with three or four. You know as well as I do that there must be about half a million on this part of the Gulf alone. All seeking compatible realtor for long-term relationship." I roughed up his barber-styled hair. I knew he didn't really want to get himself that embroiled, that responsible, or he wouldn't have moved into the garage apartment behind his folks' house after his divorce.

"Yeah." He felt around on the floor, probably in some old reflex looking for a pack of cigarettes, then flopped back on the bed. "But who wants to mess with somebody who you don't know? Who you more than likely wouldn't like. Who wants to take a chance? At my age?"

"I'll write you a reference," I said, giving him a smile.

By the time Birdie came in, having had her last private

cello lesson before school started, he and I were dressed and in the kitchen.

"Hi, Karl," my daughter greeted him politely.

"Hello, Bird. What's up?"

"We had a visit from my Uncle Rufus on Saturday."

"And here, today, is your 'Uncle Karl'?" He gave me a look that indicated I hadn't leveled with him.

Birdie let loose her shawl of hair. "He really is my uncle. Not like you."

"The head cheerleader at my high school had an Uncle Rufus. He ended up in the pen."

She giggled, heading to her room. "I know you're kidding."

"My brother-in-law," I clarified.

Karl narrowed his blue eyes as if trying to read my face. "Keep repeating that word *brother*," he said.

I laughed. After a quartet of years, we knew each other fairly well.

He helped himself to some iced coffee in the fridge, having failed to find a beer. Sitting down at the table in the other kitchen chair, he asked, "The brother-in-law want to talk about your sister?"

"He did."

"A lot of unfinished business when someone dies. That right?"

I nodded.

"Hell." He looked toward Birdie's room, in case that counted as cursing. "There's a lot of unfinished business when they don't, not to mention all this stuff still going on with my ex. But you always think you'll have time to get around to it."

"You do. You think that."

But I didn't want to talk about Red and my sister anymore. I felt saturated with the subject. I hadn't even begun to think about my promise to call some total stranger out there in cow country and tell him I hoped he was bearing up. Or how I'd felt when Red carried me across the yard in the rain. Or, for that matter, to wonder where present company, a well-meaning guy who liked to kid around with my daughter, fit in.

After he left, I fretted about Birdie. What on earth, I wondered, must it be like for her? For a girl, growing up, not to have an in-place, permanent, unchanging, postulating daddy? I couldn't even imagine my life if I'd been raised only by my mother, Agatha. It made me close my eyes and grind my teeth to think of it. Mothers, a case could be made, taught you, or felt it their duty to teach you, how to be female. How to be a member in good standing of their notion of family. But daddies—daddies gave you that sweeping, certain, pontifical view of the outside world, past, present, and forevermore. It didn't matter what the content of their world was—History repeats/History doesn't repeat; growing beef is gold on the hoof/growing beef is a crapshoot; the Law is a compass/the Law is an ass; you're entitled to a piece of anything you repo/anything you repossess belongs entirely to the original owner—you expected, growing up, to have that daddy in residence, holding forth. Just as you expected, as you came of age, to have that defining mother.

Somehow, my fault or not, I had cheated my daughter out of her due.

What had she lost growing up in a world without a daddy? Some sense of the Other. I could still shut my eyes and have the early intimate smells and sights of that bearded parent return to me. The images of his constant grooming. The mouthwash, the toothbrush, the little sets of scissors for trimming his whiskers and nose hair, his eyebrows, the finger- and toenail clippers, the pumice stone for his calluses, the almost erotic collection of prescription medicines in the bathroom cabinet, long out of date, for fevers, coughs, colds, assorted bugs. Nose sprays, eyedrops, oil for earaches, rubbing alcohol, and liniments for sore muscles. Him in the old navy cotton robe with its daddy smell that he wore before dressing, to be decent in a home with daughters. The way every act performed was accompanied by its history.

I could see him sitting on the side of his bed (their double bed), a towel spread on the floor, working on his professor's aching feet, discussing ingrown toenails and infections, plantar warts, bone spurs, bunion plasters. A world before sports shoes and podiatrists. See him leaning close to the bathroom mirror, shaving, speaking of his grandfather who'd used a straight-edged razor and leather strop, his father who'd used a mug and brush. See him working a piece of floss awkwardly between two teeth as his periodontist had taught him, reminiscing about the days of pulling teeth with pliers and a shot of whiskey, of his grandfather's false teeth in a glass beside his bed, his father's missing molars and visible gold crowns. I'm sure, if we had been sons, my sister and I, there would also have been personal talk of constipation and erections, and a recounting of the early ways of handling the problems of each.

Should I have kept Buddy about at all (substantial) cost? Just to have his Jockey shorts on the floor, his electric razor in the bathroom, neon-colored muscle shirts on every piece of furniture? The smell of aftershave, the sound of him moving around in the bedroom like an elephant behind closed doors? Just to give her an exposure to daddy, a dose of daddy, a vaccine of daddy? Big guy, proud of his build, bound to get on his only daughter about her weight, her hairy legs, why didn't she have a boyfriend, how come she was a runt just like his mother? No. No, better she have her imagined daddy, the guy in the photo with one of his temporary sailboats—great grin—calling up to ask, "How's the birdie?"

I was standing there, lost in a fog, trying to get my mind around all this, just standing, when the phone rang. I couldn't say I had a premonition—I didn't believe in them anyway—but, just as if I'd conjured him up by thinking about him, here was my daddy.

"Ella, girl," he said, his voice quavering, "we almost lost your mother."

"What, Daddy?"

But he was a flood of words. He seemed to feel that as long as he was speaking, as long as the connection held, matters were under control. "I drank a whole glass of orange juice while I waited for the ambulance, thinking to myself that there's no good to be gained with my ticker giving out while she's flat on the floor. Swallowing, I read in the Tufts Health Letter, I think it was, helps you with stress."

"Daddy, tell me what happened."

She fell, he said. As if that explained the matter.

By this time, Birdie, perhaps picking up on something in my tone of voice, had stopped practicing and come into the kitchen, so I wrote it for her on a scrap of paper: *Grandmom's in the hospital.* And she sat down by me at the round table, looking solemn.

How helpess I felt. When Terrell had been around, she would have been the one to call, to tell me exactly what had happened in swift, clear words. Tell me how to hear "she fell"; tell me what to make of it. Daddy, in his third year of retirement, had somehow retired also from the daily conversations of the outside world.

"They say she's out of the woods." He sounded at a loss. "Your mother." He made a sort of gargling sound. "We nearly lost her."

I tried to make my voice calm. "Was it a stroke, then? She had a small stroke?"

"Your mother got a letter. It was a bit of good news, at least to my way of thinking. But I suppose that's a moot matter that can wait. Good news is what it was, a letter." He stopped, then went on, as if recollecting. "Afterwards, she sat out there on the porch talking to me, most likely, I didn't hear what all, on account of working on my history, around the corner. My old ears. Then she quit and it wasn't half a minute later I heard her fall."

"Is she—" How did you ask such things? Can she hear you? Recognize you? Speak? "—all right?"

He choked up. "She kept on about your sister."

"Daddy, listen. Are you there now, the hospital? Where

are you? I could drive over tomorrow and spend a few days. How long will she——?"

Birdie took the pen and wrote: *Me, too!!!*

I tried to calculate. School started so early now; here it would start next week, three weeks before Labor Day, and it must be the same at home, students starting back in what were the crushingly hot days of August. Our noise-sensitive tenant, the elementary school teacher, Margot, had already returned and settled into her well-draining half of the house. Even Yale, Red had said, required their freshmen on-site by September 1.

Birdie added: *I can take care of Granddaddy.*

How could I deny her that?

"Do that, Daughter." Daddy sounded winded. "I'm not up to coping with trouble the way I used to."

I called Mayfair to let her know our change in plans, as much to have someone to talk to about my mother as anything else, since Birdie would of course be telling Felice the minute I got off the phone.

"It must be that generation," Mayfair said. "My aunt made a trip to look up an old teacher of hers, and when she got there, the woman could only see next of kin." She made a murmur of sympathy.

"Mother seemed indestructible."

"Don't our mamas always," she agreed.

"And our daddies——?"

"Daddies? Who's that?"

✴ Austin

16

We found Daddy, as he'd instructed, on the intensive care floor at the recently enlarged hospital not far from their house. He looked dressed to chair a departmental meeting—summer-weight navy suit, vest, starched blue shirt from his cache of blue shirts, striped yellow tie (from some Father's Day?)—and not as if he'd slept sitting up in his clothes, which, by his account, he had. When I told him he looked pretty smooth, he explained that he'd learned this trick from his brother Reuben, who'd been a judge in Ector County and said that you should never go into hospitals, law offices, or county courthouses without a tie and dress shoes, or they would decide you were an indigent—since that's what they'd been hired to do, sort the able-to-pay from the unable-to-pay.

"Guten Tag," Birdie said to him, giving him a bear squeeze.

"Hi, Girlie," he told her, looking grateful.

Waiting for it to be time to go into the ICU to see Mother, he and I sat in the hospital coffee shop, while Birdie stayed upstairs with Red and the boys. Daddy told me once again all about the study correlating swallowing with reduced stress, and, as if to test the results, drank two tall glasses of water and ate two triangles of limp toast, chewing three times longer than necessary to turn them to paste, though I didn't know if chewing was up there with swallowing. Maybe it just had to do with moving the jaw muscle, for he also talked as if her life, and maybe his, depended on it.

"I studied those health letters," he reported, "and it paid off for her. Lucky this wasn't me in there, since she hardly even scans the index. There was this article on ischemic strokes—it was in the Harvard Heart Letter or maybe the Berkeley Wellness Letter, I save the lot of them—about how minutes make the difference. You wait more than three hours, trying to figure out if maybe the person has a sinus headache or just fell asleep sitting there because the afternoon turned muggy—I'm being hypothetical here, since your mother fell—you've lost your margin of good fortune. But this is a topic people of our age, your mother and I, should keep abreast of. I'm saying this is a key topic of the older folks, and I had my data *right here*." He tapped his head and looked at me.

I could hardly sit still, much less drink even coffee. In fifteen minutes, I would see her, and the pit of my stomach felt loaded with lead. One part of me worried about her, her leaking or occluded or only grazed vessels, one part of me worried about that look of grief that I knew would cross her face. Seeing that it was only me.

"You grasp the idea, Ella? If they can give the patient, that's your mother in this case—" He waved his hand for a water refill. "But anyone, it could be me next time, the tissue plasminogen activator, they call it tPA, right away, that's the key. I asked the doctor right out, the consult, the neurosurgeon, the same thing I'd asked our usual man, 'Did I get her here in time for the tPA?' and they said I most definitely did. Though when we were waiting for that ambulance, time seemed to wobble and not move, and I had myself a bad fright."

"She's lucky to have you, Daddy." I tried to pull myself together.

"Your mother has been under a lot—I'm not sure you understand—been through a lot of stress."

Riding the elevator upstairs beside him, I found myself short of breath, my hands clammy. Trying his remedy, I made myself swallow. My mother, I feared, flat on her back, her body having misbehaved, would be even more in control than ever, to compensate. I'd left Old Metairie, driving like crazy for most of the day, in the same café au lait sleeveless dress I'd worn with Red, minus the black T-shirt, which I'd thrown into the bag with my best watering shorts and a pull-on black-and-blue synthetic skirt from some previous incarnation. Where had all the linens, hanging in the closet of my mind, gone? Where the manicured nails, the soft French braid? I had arrived looking exactly what I was: the out-of-state, out-of-favor, and out-of-funds remaining daughter.

Going into the waiting room, I tried to prepare myself for seeing Red again. Wanting not to make too much out of what happened last weekend in Old Metairie. He'd wanted information; I'd supplied it. Still, I'd sat in my small blue front room late each night, waiting for the eleven o'clock train, thinking about him. How much I'd liked him back then; how much I found I liked him now. How totally impossible anything more developing between us was.

"Hello, Rufus," I said, and felt a moment of shame that I was so glad to see him, that maybe the reason I'd leapt at the chance to drive my brains out to get to Mother's bedside was the fact that he'd be here, too.

"Hello, Ella." He flushed.

We stood rooted a second, awkward, before reaching out at the same time for a handshake. I'm sure, if we hadn't had the time in my territory, if he'd really been only Birdie's uncle, I'd have offered my cheek for a kin-kiss, he'd have given me a familial hug. I wondered if our children sensed this new unease between their parents. Wondered, also, what he'd said to his boys about his trip.

"Hi, Uncle Rufus," Birdie said loudly, making everything seem natural. "I came to take care of Granddaddy."

"That's good."

"Hi, Aunt Ella," Borden and Bailey said at the same time. Both were dressed as if for church, in blazers with shirts and ties, pressed slacks. Both also wore running shoes, perhaps on the theory that no one in a hospital bed would be looking at your feet. They'd risen when Daddy and I came into the cozy intensive care waiting room, where the half dozen other visitors sat reading *People, Newsweek, Texas Monthly,* appearing to be managing, hanging in.

Then the nurse signaled me, and I followed her into the

ICU, to the glassed-in room where my mother lay partially propped up in bed.

"Hello, Mother," I said, tucking my hair behind my ears in order to look neater when I leaned toward her.

"It's Ella, isn't it?" Her voice sounded hoarse, as if she'd had a tube down her throat.

"Yes, Mother. It's me."

"They think I don't know Terrell is gone." She had an IV taped in the back of her hand, and wires monitoring her. "But I do. Apparently I tried to explain to the doctor what a sweet baby she was, such a pretty thing, and worth it after all." She made a faint smile. She wore a hospital gown and her hair had been brushed for visitors, but flattened and parted on the wrong side, the auburn color faded. Someone had even applied some of her own coral lipstick to her mouth, but in a too-thick, overgenerous manner. No wonder sick people did not look themselves. Her breath had a faint metallic odor.

"You look good," I told her, in a clumsy attempt to be positive. "Your color is good."

"Time gets—scrambled—when you lose a snippet. I was back there somewhere." Her voice was weak, but she looked in good spirits, somehow younger.

"I'm glad you're here." I reached up a hand to twist my hair back. What a dunce. I hadn't meant *here,* in the hospital, I'd meant—

"I don't know, dear, the present is overrated." She again smiled, with effort. Then, shutting her eyes, waved me away. "That's enough for now," she whispered.

Outside her room, the nurse checked her monitor, one

of a row of monitors, each with an undulating line. Back in the waiting room, Daddy was explaining to his grandchildren that the first three days were the danger period, that sometimes things went wrong after a stroke at that time, like a stretched rubber band snapping back. Birdie stood by his side.

"How is she?" Red asked.

"She's——" I couldn't find the words. Her tone had been different, girlish. "——Quite lucid."

The cousins stood in a clump, waiting to go in. Borden, once tall as my daddy, now taller by a bit, looked panicked. He reached up a hand to smooth back his hair. "What do you say in there, Aunt Ella? Dad? What are we supposed to *say*?"

What, indeed, to one's grandmother in intensive care. "Tell her—tell her she looks good," I instructed.

Daddy made a few deep sounds. He seemed worn out but not yet wound down, and refused to sit, waiting for his turn to go in again. "I'm getting into gear to start walking," he told me and the waiting room at large. "You can bet this scare with your mother waved a red flag where the two of us are concerned."

"You must be thirsty," I suggested.

"Swallowing——" He looked around, anxious, as if for a water fountain.

I located four quarters and sent him to the machines past the nurse's station.

Alone, Red and I found a small upholstered sofa and sat, watching the doorway. "Your dad's holding up," he said.

"You think? He hasn't stopped talking——"

He looked around the room. "This place wipes me out.

My dad used to be a regular, in the old wing. First he broke his thigh bone, falling off a ladder, and was mad as an ox till it healed, then he got blood poisoning, which the doctor, a kid just out of Baylor Med, had never seen a case of, then his heart wore out. My mom gave up on him, so I was the one who came around." He smiled at me. "I'm glad to see you, even in this not-so-great surrounding."

"I'm glad to see you."

"I started to call a dozen times."

"I wish you had."

"I didn't know what to say."

I nodded.

"I didn't know where we'd left it—" He looked a question at me.

"You got what you came for." I tried to sound as if that was fine.

He was in a white shirt, the sleeves rolled up, looking much as he had when he'd driven away from my house. "True. Some validation that it wasn't all my fault."

"Oh, Red, it always takes two to mess things up."

He met my eyes. "This isn't the right place, and your dad's in no shape to consider the idea, but I'd like to come courting." He smiled at using the old-fashioned term.

I drew in my breath, caught unaware. Pleasure swept over me. Keeping my voice steady, I suggested, "I guess at our age, we have to ask the children." I watched a woman supported by two younger women pass by in the hall.

"I'm asking you."

"But how can we—see each other, that way?" Though I so much wanted to, to be back in that car with Red, leaning against the door, in that space with no one else there, everything easy, him close enough to touch, talking about things we couldn't tell anyone else. Past that? Past that, I couldn't let myself think. The idea of telling my mother that Terrell's fine husband was seeing Terrell's scruffy younger sister, that I could presume to have designs on my sister's man, the father of her fine children. I shut my eyes at the thought. Seeing her face propped up on the pillow in ICU, her hair too flat, her mouth out of boundaries, a mother I never knew, back in a happier time.

"I don't know," Red said. "But I'd like to try."

"Your boys?"

His eyes watched the door. "The boys and I had a talk. I told them, after the crash, that I'd rent out the house, her house, their house, for a year, and then we could sell it and put the money into their education, or we could hold it for them to live in. When I came back from seeing you, both told me, 'Sell it, Dad.' I think they could see they weren't going to go back, just the two of them, once they were out of school."

"That's tough for them, dealing with that."

"For all of us."

Then the children swarmed into the waiting room, looking keyed up but relieved to have paid their proper respects to their grandmother. Past them, in the hall, I saw the nurse snag my daddy and lead him into intensive care.

Borden, his handsome fair head bobbing up and down, wanting to report, said, "I told her, like you said, Aunt Ella. I told her, 'You look good, Grandmom,' and, sort of, she did—"

Bailey interrupted, his jacket hanging loose on his thin frame, his cowlick turned skyward. "She said she had a picture of us, on her desk at home."

Birdie stood on tiptoe, hair tied back, between the two tall cousins, adding her part. "Grandma said, 'Imagine, I started all this family,' the first thing, when we walked into her room."

Then the trio fell silent when Daddy stumbled in, gazing all around. His face streaked, an open can of orange juice in his hand, he came toward us.

"Hey," I said, rising and putting my arms around his heaving chest. "Hey, there. Come sit down."

The tears soaked into his thick beard as he sank onto the small public sofa. "Your mother asked me just now, looking square at me, 'Wasn't she the most beautiful baby, ever?' "

17

I couldn't have imagined a house more different in every way from the one where my sister had lived for most of her married life than the one Red had moved into with his sons. He'd given me directions, penned on the back of a hospital napkin—out I-35 north to Farm-to-Market 1825 east—and I found the limestone house with little difficulty, in the old part of Pflugerville where, he said, there hadn't been a new real estate listing in decades. Places having been handed down in families for a century, farming families not about to sell to strangers. And I could see that to my nephews, used to the luxurious hills, woods, lake in West Lake Hills, their relocation to what in my day had been just a tiny German wide-spot-in-the-road must have seemed an exile to the ultimate boonies. But then, in my day, that parcel of land where Red had moved his life wasn't yet the hub of a techno-strip that stretched in all directions, bringing whole new communities with it. It was just a little burg that published a weekly newspaper called the *Pflugerville Pflag*.

Standing on the wide porch, Birdie at my side, arriving as invited for an early supper, Daddy still keeping watch at the hospital, I tried to imagine Terrell here. Terrell driving here, walking in the still-baking, early-evening heat across the rocky yard through a stand of live oaks. It stopped me in my tracks. I could not envision her ever setting foot on this ground. And wondered if that fact, her total absence here, was a relief to the boys. Or, if, instead, it made the place unbearable.

"You found your way," Red said, opening the door to the cool stone house.

"I used to come out here, to Pflugerville."

"In school?"

"Beer drinking in some dance hall with Buddy. Don't tell my folks." It didn't seem all that long ago: I was dressed the same, in a long skirt, and my hair was the same, wild.

"If you won't tell them I live here."

"Too late."

"Uncle Rufus," Birdie said, "I brought something for supper."

"No fair. We're having barbeque."

She laughed. "Not to *eat*. That would be bad manners. This is like a, you know, present you bring if you're having supper at somebody's house." She'd worn her Amish dress, which she'd packed, along with her best baggy shorts, for our trip. At home, she'd asked did she have to bring the awful elephant-gray jumper, then she'd asked me if I was going to take my green linen dress, the dress she'd worked so hard to help me find at the thrifts. When I claimed I'd lost it, she said, "Okay." A good daughter, knowing when not to ask questions.

Red sent her back to the kitchen to find the boys, then he and I stood a minute while I looked around the vast living room, with its old four-person sofa, four stuffed chairs, a rug or two. It could have been someone's grandparents' house in the Hill Country. "They hate this, don't they?" I asked him.

"They do." He'd changed to jeans and a T-shirt, and could, I thought, in his wire-rim glasses, with his cropped dark hair, have just come back from Dell or Compaq or IBM or Texas Instruments. All he lacked was the pocket full of pens. "Borden is counting the days till he leaves."

"And Bailey?"

He shook his head. "He says no way he's commuting an hour a day to graduate West Lake Hills High and no way he's going to transfer to P-f-Pfucking Pfluggie, as he calls the local school." He looked dejected. "If he drops out, I have to hold myself responsible." He shoved his hands in his pockets.

I crossed my arms, still awkward with him, still very aware of the two of us alone, talking of real matters. This evening, we had held back from even shaking hands. "In hindsight," I asked, "should you have stayed in West Lake Hills for his last year?"

"I wasn't *there* when she died. I'd moved. It wasn't a matter of staying. Should I have moved back in? Should I have moved my stuff into that bedroom we'd shared? Eaten at that dining table? Been reminded every day?"

I shrugged and smiled. "Probably."

"Sure, probably. In hindsight." He seemed somewhat cheered, just to talk about it. "Anyway, we can still find you a beer out here in the sticks."

"Good. On the bayou we serve only white wine." I was still hugging my own arms, like a girl on a first date.

He led me on a tour of the house on the way to the fridge. He pointed out a leak in the roof, one of three left from his daddy's day, although not a problem in a rainless era, a couple of ancient but functional bathrooms, three musty oak-floored bedrooms with solid oak doors, a kitchen with no amenities except vast space, a rear porch once used for churning butter and for storing the wringer washing machine. And, out back, in the cleared yard away from the shade of cottonwoods, pecans, and sycamores, away from a low-growing catalpa, a stand of pink, purple, and red hollyhock blooming away in the bone-dry twilight.

In the dining area opening off the kitchen (a space bigger than my front sitting room), the boys lounged with Birdie seated between them. Like mannerly males, they rose, then sat again when I entered the room. Borden, in navy cargo pants and a navy polo, Bailey, in khaki cargo pants and polo, with a matching bucket cap. All their clothes from Abercrombie, so my daughter had reported. I wondered if they had girlfriends? Surely, at their age. But what did I know about boys who had all the accomplishments and achievements it took to get into the Ivies? Terrell hadn't mentioned girl or even guy friends, just their sports records, their academic honors. To me, now, their body language unmistakably said: We're truly pissed to have ended up here.

Taking my longneck, icy cold, I tarried behind Red, who'd gone back into the living room. Lingering in the wide hall so common to old houses, I eavesdropped a bit.

"I'm having a Dutch beer and pica-brain here is having a Mexican beer, but we can't serve you one, because you're only fourteen." This was Bailey speaking to my daughter.

Birdie answered, "That's all right. I'm not a beer drinker anyway." I imagined her lifting her immense fan of frizzy hair. "I like orange juice, and if you don't have that, I like Snapple." She paused, then said, "My mom drinks iced coffee."

"She asked for a Lone Star."

"Then I guess she's having a date with your daddy."

"She's not having a date with our dad, Birdie." Borden's voice rose. "She can't, because she's our mom's——," he stammered. "Was our mom's sister. That's *incest*."

"No, it isn't, or my mom wouldn't do it." Birdie made a noise as if moving her chair. "Who's cooking supper?" She changed the subject.

"Nobody cooks here." Borden sounded glum.

"Nano-brain means that we buy stuff and bring it home." She explained, "I cook lunch on the weekend at my house, and my mom cooks supper. That's what we do at our house."

Wandering out of earshot, I joined Red on the wide sofa, tucking my long blue-and-black skirt behind my legs.

"And the topic was——?" he asked.

"Whether it's incest if we're having a date."

He looked away. "Ouch."

"I know."

We rose, not looking at one another, in unspoken agreement, I suppose, that sitting alone on the sofa drinking beer was not a great idea. "Want to see what I'm working on?" he asked.

"Very much."

Following, I told him that Daddy had gone home with us, got changed into another starched blue shirt, and another yellow tie, and gone back. That they were moving Mother to a private room tomorrow. That he wouldn't hear of leaving her and would spend the night, as before, in the waiting room.

"I'll stop back by to see him. The logistics of Borden's leaving have slowed me down."

"Will he fly?"

He sighed, talking to the air in front of him, me trailing behind. "If he flies, I have to crate up all his essential possessions; if we drive, I can load up the car." He brushed that away with his hand.

We went into what must, in his parents' day, have been the master bedroom, the room where his mom and dad slept. It had windows on the front of the house, through which we could see the stepping-stones and, past the front yard, two cars going slowly by. On the east wall, facing us as we came into the room, he had a blowup of the famous sixties Valley Citrus Workers march. The men (all men) in work pants, wrinkled shirts, bandanas tied around their necks to keep off the sun, worn shoes, carrying (at least for the newspaper photo) banners. On the north wall, facing the front windows, he had a similar blowup of a group of men and women, mostly Mexican in appearance, some Anglo, at computers, their screens detailing wages and hours at the orchards. Around the walls he had computer stations and chairs.

"Who works here?" I asked him.

"I've got a computer whiz borrowed from Dell, Chinese woman, who's training a core group to go to the plantations and teach the workers."

I made a slow turn around the room. "Where are the oranges?"

"Oranges?"

I was thinking of seasonal workers like myself, untrained workers who learned on the job. Of gardeners like Henry, whose hands and eyes "knew" the plants he tended, knew how to dig those trenches to drain them, how to breed them and feed them, who knew their family histories back to Eden. And who taught me. "You remember the head rose gardener at Belle Vue," I said.

"Henry, right? I guess I envied him a bit, his work."

"Well, if you were talking about Henry, you'd have to talk about *roses,* how much he loved roses. The same way that these gardeners must love *oranges.* Must be able to shut their eyes and tell from the smell and feel of the fruit what kind of orange they're holding." I thought of old roses the color of mandarin oranges, and then of tangerines, of clementines, of marmalades, of perfumes made from the precious bergamot oranges of Italy and Spain, of orange-blossom weddings in the Rio Grande Valley. "Think about that killing freeze of eighty-nine," I reminded him, "the orange gardeners covering the trees with tarps, putting those little smudgy pots under the wraps. And then losing not just the fruit, but losing every tree. One by one the trees dying at the roots. And then losing their jobs. Think of Henry, if all his roses died. If he had no roses and no job."

"I hadn't thought of that," Red said. "Each one a Henry." He turned out the light, checked that everything was shut down. Outside, in the dry dusk, the oaks cast long shadows on the parched, rocky ground.

"This is exciting work," I told him, "what you're doing."

"I don't want to talk about how my wife wouldn't hear about it. How she'd leave the room, slam the door. How she kept the house filled with people to avoid the issue."

"I don't want to, either, Red, talk about my sister. I don't want her here, in this room."

"She isn't here. She never set foot in this house, even when my folks were alive. She put them on a dairy farm, my grandparents' dairy farm, near the Blue Bell Creamery."

"Upgraded them."

"For Agatha."

"I guess we all remade ourselves for Mother." I felt a hot burning in my throat, not tears, but their echo. It had never ever dawned on me that Terrell, too, the favored daughter, had felt compelled to falsify portions of her life.

"Ella, I want to think of you the way I knew you twenty-five years ago, a high school girl I felt embarrassed to be attracted to. I want to pretend I kept up with you through your family, and then ran into you again this summer."

I knotted my hands together and turned to him. "I wish it had been that way," I admitted. "I wish I hadn't seen you since we ate those grubby hamburgers and then one day you showed up at my door—" I bit my lip. "But you heard the children."

"I got their message." He sighed.

I turned to him then, and put my hand on his cheek, and, in the dim light, his face felt familiar, known. I put my mouth on his and parted my lips, our bodies not touching, his hands braced on the shelf behind him. I kissed him until I felt his tongue, and then drew awkwardly away.

In the kitchen, afraid to get too close, we opened another beer and talked about his plans for the old house, about how my plumbing was doing in Old Metairie, cooling down until the kids reappeared with our supper. They'd gone to fetch it in Red's car, and I gathered Birdie had got to have a say in the selection but not a veto. As they hauled the sacks and cartons in, I heard Bailey grumbling that if he had to live out here with the cedar-choppers, he at least ought to have a pickup, and inferred he wouldn't hate driving a truck.

I couldn't believe the food. If I'd shut my eyes and waved my hands to make my dream meal appear, this would have been it. Slabs of beef barbeque and spicy pork ribs, from Tuffy's Bar-B-Q, Borden said, very tasty and chewy, and from Dodge City Steakhouse, Bailey's choice, a double order of fried chicken livers and gizzards, plus Birdie's pick, three small peach cobblers and one large coconut butter-milk chess pie, which she cut into five equal slices. Too much. Actually, not too much at all. I had thirds, along with the boys, and then Red and I moved into the kitchen proper to make a pot (perk pot) of coffee.

And to listen a bit to our young.

"So what do you want to be, Borden?" Birdie asked. "I mean, that's great about Yale and all. So you must have a lot of ambitions."

Her older cousin made a few throat-clearing noises, then responded without a lot of conviction. "I may get an M.B.A. Mom—Mom said you could go in a lot of directions with an M.B.A. But I haven't decided for sure. I may do law school. Dad says that you can go a lot of different ways with a law degree."

"Do you want to go in a lot of different directions?" Birdie sounded like that was okay, if he did.

"I don't know. Mostly, duh." He cleared his throat. "Mostly I wanted to get my acceptance letter."

"What about you, Bailey?" Birdie, my daughter, the gracious conversationalist.

"I guess I'll probably, more than likely, I suppose, drop out for now."

"A lot of guys do that," she told him. "Computer guys. They don't even do college."

"I'm not into computers," Bailey said. "I'm just— ummmm—I'm just going to take some time off?"

"From what?"

"I mean, I'm going to investigate my options." His voice rose with anxiety. "Maybe help Dad out with his fruit pickers or something. I guess, probably."

"While you live at your daddy's house and he pays for your Abercrombie clothes with his credit card? That's not dropping out, Bailey."

He leaned across the table in her face. "I don't want to go to school *here* and I can't go back over *there,* where all my, where everybody—"

Borden smoothed back his hair, looking guilty. "Listen, dumbo, just be *somewhere* so you can get your applications in."

"What do you know? You're going off. You don't have to stay in this—this fleabag town."

I imagined him spelling it in his mind: *pfleabag.* Beside me, Red hunched his shoulders, intent on watching the percolator perk.

"Here's the thing," Birdie said, as if she could help by informing him, "about school. You don't go to school because of who's at your school, you go to school to find out what you already know. You find out that half the people there are ninety-five percent smarter than you. So what's the five percent you have over them? That's what you go to school for, to see what you have that's special."

Bailey finished off the last bite of his coconut buttermilk chess pie and half rose out of his seat. "You are a dumb, dumpy girl with hairy legs. *What do you know?*"

Red moved as if to whack his son across the face, but I held him back. Our children were treating each other like siblings, something my daughter sorely needed and maybe his boys did, too. I wasn't worried about Birdie taking care of herself.

Standing up, she announced, as if it was time, as if her cousin wasn't sitting there glowering at her, "I brought us something for after supper. Our granddaddy let me pick it out from the CDs in his library. I like this a whole lot. It's Brahms's Double Concerto for Violin and Cello in A minor, and the cello player, Mstislav Rostropovich, who plays with Itzhak Perlman, is the best ever. I guess you know that's what I play? In the String Project?" She looked at the boys, and in her loudest voice said, "And someday I'm going to play like that."

Borden, ever polite, unfolded himself from his chair and showed her where the CD player was. And then all three of them sat, sprawled, and we joined them with our coffee, no one making a sound. Clear through to the last movement. By which time we had all lost ourselves in the heart-plucking strings that filled the old rooms of Red's daddy's house in Pflugerville.

18

Daddy fixed us a big breakfast, bacon, two eggs each, for Birdie and me, also him. English muffins with berry jam, since Mother wasn't up to baking her sweet-milk biscuits. He told us again how butter was back; did I know men had more strokes on oleo? He couldn't remember what he'd said before, only that the good news was he had his wife home, and, thanks to his careful reading of all health bulletins, she would soon be good as new. Good as before, he amended.

He wore his favorite bedroom slippers, worn down at the heels, felt-lined, but showed us proudly a shoebox containing his new Topsiders, the leather boat shoes with hard-rubber soles supposed to be better for old feet to walk in. What did I think?

I told him they looked good, were a good idea. Maybe he was going to start walking around the block?

"One of these days," he agreed. "I'm getting set."

Birdie thanked him for the Brahms concerto, and he said he set a lot of store by somebody who knew what was what, as far as music was concerned. Though at one time, his daughter Terrell——. He clouded up, looked away, but then turned his attention to matters at hand. "You go have a listen now, Girlie," he told his granddaughter. "I have a little matter to discuss with your mother. Pull the door to."

"Okay," Birdie said, wiping her mouth, thrilled to be sent off with full liberty to explore the music. She gave her granddaddy a massive throat-choke hug before she left.

"Daughter," Daddy began, not getting up to clear the plates, a clue that he had something on his mind. "I need to broach a certain matter with you. The hospital, as you know, not being a proper surrounding for personal matters."

I felt something go flip-flop in my middle. Was he going to talk about Red? Had he, somehow, seen something between us the day I arrived? Had he, being, after all, my daddy, picked up on a new distractedness, heard something in my tone when I told him what a fine feast we'd had with his grandsons at their daddy's house? I blushed despite myself. "Is everything all right?"

He dug out his reading glasses from the pocket of his blue shirt. "You may recall my mentioning, when we had that scare about your mother, that she'd got what was, to my way of reasoning, good news."

I had to shift my thinking, still with damp palms, a dry mouth, trying to decide, if confronted, what I would, or could tell him. "When you called——" I did recall his saying my mother had got—some news. But I'd been frantic to find out what exactly had happened to her. "——You might have——"

"I think you ought to be brought into this matter," he said, "included in what is, you might say, family history."

And then I thought, somehow, that he had his will or rather their will on his mind. Mother's stroke, her likelihood of another. Perhaps some trust he had in mind.

He walked into his study and returned with a leather folder, from which he produced a letter on thick white paper. But even when he showed me the envelope, addressed to AGATHA ADAMS HOPKINS, I still didn't get it. My mind, in fact, went back to the hanky letter, and I wondered if this were something from that time in her life. When I just sat there, not sure what I was supposed to do, he opened it for me. "Here," he said, "this came for your mother, the day she—fell."

I read, but the first time, nothing registered.

Dear Mrs. Hopkins (although it is most difficult not to address you as Miss Adams),

I'm writing to inform you that my sister, whom you will remember as your student Molly Clark, has recently become principal of the little school where you taught. You may not know that your preschool program, which meant so much to all of us in Angelina County at a turning point in our young lives nearly fifty years ago, has been incorporated into the kindergarten program today.

It is my sister's wish, on her first public occasion, to celebrate the past of the school with an AGATHA ADAMS DAY in your honor. I will call on you in person in the coming week, to answer any of your questions, but

we hope you will be pleased, and that your health is such
that you can be present at this landmark event.
Sincerely yours,
Your former student,
Sadie Clark (Grimes)

I looked up at Daddy.

"Your mother took this hard, harder than I saw at the time. I have myself to blame, going on with my desk work, not understanding her upset."

"This came to Mother?" I tried to clear my head. "Mother was a teacher?"

"When we met, indeed she was, a fine inspiration to her young charges. Hard to believe—fifty years." He tugged at his beard, looking puzzled. So much time gone by.

I tried to get my mind around it. Agatha, the nice girl from the nice family in sleepy, southern East Texas, the girl who collected lace-trimmed hankies from her pen friends, and sachets, and valentines. "I didn't know," I said. Had Terrell? I tried to picture her, the woman who became my mother, as Miss Adams, in a nice lilac linen dress, a lace-edged handkerchief in her pocket for drying childish tears, serving juice and cookies to the children of her hanky friends. Perhaps it was a churchy job, something they took turns doing.

"She's not one for bringing up the matter." Daddy sighed and scratched his head.

"It was this letter, this fine honor, that upset her?" Had she not wanted to be reminded of small girls such as the letter writer, Sadie, and her sister, Molly? Had that brought back the years when she had two small girls herself? Perhaps one of these students had been a favorite. Little blond girl in a sundress.

"Being reminded of the past is a disservice, you might say, in the view of your mother."

"What can I do?" I asked him.

"I got myself into a bucket of hot water here, I'm afraid," Daddy confessed, retrieving the letter and returning it to the folder. "I promised that woman, Mrs. Grimes, who is making the trip to Austin expressly to see your mother and deliver her invitation in person, that she is welcome to come by our home this coming Friday morning, although naturally she did not wish to impose at this time." He looked at me, his pale face stricken. "Do you reckon you and your girl could delay a couple of days, stay the weekend?"

Daddy's hands shook a bit as he tried to stack our plates. I always forgot, for all his talk about his diet, and his general medical savvy, that, at seventy-five, he led a sedentary and a stressful life.

"I don't know——" I said. How would Birdie take that? Missing the opening days of school—Thursday and Friday—when everyone flocked back and got their classrooms? Yet the idea of having a reason to stay, of seeing Red again and having, perhaps, a chance to figure out if there was any way, if we had a right, if we could be anything to each other, overwhelmed me. "If Birdie agrees. It's her say."

"Let me talk to her," he proposed.

Just then we heard Mother making her way slowly down the sunporch. "Judah?" she called. "I thought I might have a cup of tea, if you wouldn't mind?"

"In here," he answered, lumbering to his feet. All but dropping our plates. "You shouldn't have tried, by yourself. Here, let me—" He held out an arm to her. "I was visiting with our daughter while she ate."

"Ella," Mother said, looking down, her tone flat. "Oh, yes." She let herself be settled into a chair with a cup of tea and lemon. She'd done her own hair, and wore an apricot silk robe and slippers. Except that she was a little short of breath, her skin a little sallow, she looked herself again. Controlled, sad. The girlishness of her hospital stay vanished.

She began a yard story, a distraction for herself, if not for us. "Did I tell you, Ella, about my encounter with the new dog across the street? Last week, it must have been—" She took a sip of tea. "Yes, before—my fall. It belongs to the young couple, he's a banker, who fixed up the Prather place? I'd been watching it for days, a wiry black dog, I don't know the breed. They have so many these days, you never see cocker spaniels anymore. Well, it's been trained to chase after a soft sort of Frisbee, that looks almost like a cloth watermelon slice. It's nothing short of amazing, I have to say, the way that dog can run down the lawn, no matter how far the toy is thrown, and catch it in its mouth—" She paused, short of breath.

"Mother," I interrupted, before she could go further, knowing that once she got into it, the account running like a home movie before her eyes, I'd never get to speak. "That's quite wonderful, your old school having an Agatha Adams Day. You must be quite pleased."

She stopped short and stared at me. Shaking her head as if

to clear it, she frowned. "I suppose your father couldn't keep the news to himself." She looked at Daddy, a forced smile on her lips. Indicating the slim reading glasses tucked in the pocket of her robe, she said, "I was just composing a proper thank-you to that school principal for her kind gesture, when I thought to have a cup of tea. Although I'm sure there were many more significant teachers in her later life."

"That's quite an honor," I told her, still trying to reach that earlier woman, setting out fingerpaints for preschoolers, blowing sniffly noses, tying the sashes on pinafores.

"I was half your age, Ella," she snapped, "a girl not looking to the future."

Daddy reached out a broad hand and attempted to pat her shoulder. "It seems to me," he suggested, "that our daughter could act as a sort of surrogate hostess when Mrs. Grimes comes to call. I was enlisting her help. It mustn't be a strain for you. Your task is to take it easy for a spell."

"That woman is *not coming here*." Mother stood, holding on to the back of her chair.

"Sweetheart, if you remember, we already agreed to give her a few minutes, and put the matter to rest. I consider that a courtesy, on account of she is fetching herself all the way from Angelina County to call upon you. And most certainly they can't expect you to make that trip under the present circumstances—"

"I have never gone back there and I never will. As far as I am concerned, and you are concerned, Judah, my present life began with our marriage and the birth of our first daughter." She turned on her heel, giving the chair a sharp shove. Her voice catching, she added, "And that is no business of Ella's."

"Hello, Grandmother," Birdie said, coming in from Daddy's study in her baggy shorts, her hair about her shoulders. "How are you feeling?"

Mother waved her away with a hand. "Robin, dear, you needn't feel you have to listen to an old woman. I'm sure you'd prefer to enjoy your grandfather's music." She pulled herself together, squaring her shoulders and patting her hair. Looking at me, she said in an amused tone, "That little dog dashed across the street and dropped the Frisbee at my feet, so I could have a throw. Wasn't that the dearest thing?"

19

Late that afternoon, I called Red from the upstairs phone at Mother's, nervous as a goose. It felt exactly the way it had the first time I sat here and called a boy in high school, my palms sweaty, my chest heaving, notes on the bedspread of what I was going to say. My voice raspy from practicing my opening: Hi, this is Ella. Hi, is this _____? Hello, I was calling _____. Hello?

But when he answered, all I said was, "Red?"

"Ella," he said, "hello." His voice had a bit of a high school touch itself. Perhaps he'd been talking to the mirror in the bathroom: Hel-lo, El-la.

The idea made me smile. I took a deep breath and lay on my back on the bed, my legs crossed, swinging one foot. "Is this a bad time?"

"No, actually, I'm working on something I want you to see."

"I'm staying the weekend, as it turns out."

"You are?" His voice lifted. "Is everything okay?"

"Mother's doing better, but I'm a bit unglued. I'll tell you."

"You want to get coffee?"

"Could you in the morning, late?"

"Anytime." He definitely sounded glad.

I looked at my sheet of paper which had a single entry: *Mr. Emu.* I thought of him, Terrell's man, waiting in the sleet. "Tell me," I said, "how to call the guy on the runway?"

After a pause, he said, "You don't have to do that."

"We agreed." And we had, on a rainy night in my car.

He gave me the basic information: his name was listed as Everett Rowland, everyone but the phone company called him Skip, he had a couple of ranches, one somewhere near Sweetwater, one in the vicinity of his dad's holdings close to Odessa. His home was on a spread outside Buda, a small community west of Austin, with a post office, drugstore, and Czech bakery.

"Where will you call from?" Red asked.

"Oh." It had not occurred to me to think that through. Of course I didn't want some unidentified number on Daddy's bill, in case it showed up as an out-of-the-area call. I suggested a pay phone, but could see how non-casual that would be, on some street corner, feeding quarters to a black box.

"You want to come here?" he offered.

"That's too—awkward."

"I'll give you my card number."

"Then it'll show up on your phone bill."

"Ella, I *have* the number. I just looked it up for you."

"Sorry. I'm not too calm."

"About this?"

"And over here."

"Should I stop by to pay my respects?"

"Don't," I said, and gazed up at my foot. We were okay on the phone. Pretty relaxed. I imagined him stepping out of the Citrus Workers network room and maybe leaning against the counter in the kitchen. I wondered if he pictured me up here, in this tree-shaded room on the bed. Had he been allowed upstairs when he'd been courting Terrell? It made me think we could talk at night when I got back to Old Metairie; I could call him from the small front room, after the eleven o'clock train went by.

"Do you remember Cisco's bakery?" he asked.

"Sure. In East Austin."

"Meet me there in the morning."

"Late. Eleven. No kids."

He laughed. "No kids. Can we handle that?"

"I'm scared."

"So am I," he said, "but not about the livestock guy."

"Him, too."

I told my daddy I had to run some errands. He and Birdie were busying themselves with supper. Let him think I had to buy some personal product; all that females had to say to daddies was "some shopping" and avert their eyes to be sent on their way. The call didn't turn out to be that difficult. I went to Central Market—thinking, I guess, of Terrell—and used an outside phone, under a deep overhang, out of the searing late-afternoon sun. From where I stood, I could see the sprinklers trying to make an oasis out of the star-shaped wildflower garden at Central Park.

"Is this—Skip?" I asked the male voice that answered.

"Who's this?" he asked back, in such a wide West Texas twang I nearly reeled.

"This is Ella Hopkins." I hesitated. Should I say Terrell's name?

"The sister," he said right off. "You're the sister."

"Yes, I am." So we'd got past that hurdle.

"You here, or what?"

"I'm here, in Austin. Mother had a small stroke."

"No wonder, from what I heard."

"No, I suppose not." My tongue felt tied.

"I reckon your sister talked about me."

With relief, I said, "She did. When you—before the New Orleans trip."

"That's right. Elly. No wonder the name rang a bell."

"I wanted to call you."

He coughed, cleared his throat. "How about if we get together? While you're here. A good opportunity, seems to me. I have a natural curiosity."

I nodded, looking around at the stream of people leaving with sacks full of supper. "So have I."

"You got a place in mind? I'm flexible. I got nothing to hide, running into you, nobody here knows."

"I'm at Central Market, do you know where—" It came to me then, standing not too far from the live-oak-shaded deck where I'd had a pastry with my sister, that no doubt they'd met here. Where better to "run into" someone, where everyone must shop before the sailing weekend, the whitewing hunting weekend, the tennis tournament weekend?

"I been there."

"Outside, at one of the tables? Tomorrow morning? Nine o'clock?" I could hear the anxiety in my voice as a panic came over me. What on earth was I doing, setting up this meeting?

"Suits me." He didn't sound bothered. "You look like her?"

"Not much." Scrawnier, drabber, plainer. Not hardly. I had to laugh. "Not a bit, Skip. But I'll be there, in a black T-shirt, a nervous wreck."

He laughed then himself, ranch-country laugh. "Don't be expecting some big stud, now, Elly. Terry had an inflated view of me." He choked up on her name. "She didn't happen to show you a picture?"

"No."

"Let me give it some thought, here. How about if, shoot, this frying-pan weather." He paused. "How about if I wear my NOTREES cap? Can't be much of a duplication there."

So I found myself totally at ease about the meeting with Mr. Emu. I'd tell him anything he might want to know about my sister. I'd be an ear for him to pour out some of his feelings into. And then I'd tell Red enough that he could close the matter in his own mind.

The next morning, I got myself looking decent and told Birdie that I was meeting Red and his Chinese techie to learn about his new project, that the boys were sorting things for Yale. Daddy, stewing around about the woman coming, thanked me for squaring it with Birdie's principal and told me to fill my car up with gas, on him, for the return trip home and pressed his Mobil card in my hand. I don't know what Mother thought about my absence, if she did; she'd scarcely appeared since yesterday, only to have some orange juice.

I parked, got us two cups of coffee at the outside bakery, and, in my best watering shorts and the black tee, headed for the tables on Central Market's outside deck.

It wasn't too much of an exaggeration to say that when I caught sight of Skip Rowland I almost fell down in a dead faint. I could feel my heart begin to operate in double-time. I couldn't catch my breath. Holy Moly, shit, quick a wooden stake, I was looking at the spitting image of Buddy Marshall. The last snapshot I'd had of Buddy, taken half a dozen years ago, he was in his wraparound shades, a cap on, T-shirt with a pack of cigarettes tucked up one sleeve, wearing a monster grin. But the same exact look as this guy, sitting there in a tight burnt-orange T-shirt with a longhorn on it, and a cap that read I LOVE NOTREES. I thought of Red saying that he remembered Buddy: big old hunk, lots of macho moves. No wonder he'd felt stabbed to learn the lover was this man—the last guy in the world you'd want to know was having it with your wife.

"That you?" He half rose from the bench.

"That's me," I acknowledged, setting our coffee on the table. "Ella Hopkins." Sitting down, I kept hearing bells go off. Not bells meaning I wanted any part of a return engagement with this type, but bells thinking about my sister. Hearing her say half a dozen times through the years: "I never had that, what you had with Buddy. I never was head over heels with anybody like that."

"I sure appreciate you making that phone call," he said, removing his cap and wiping the sweat off his forehead. He took off his shades, too, and I could see that, naturally, his eyes were blue. While I sat there, somewhat numb, he went and got us a couple of hot donuts, and then, while I was grasping for something, anything, to say, he began to talk.

"The thing about Terry"—he leaned over in a confidential manner—"was you could talk to her about real stuff and she didn't interrupt or get busy doing something else the way my wife, the way some women, a lot of women, it seems to me, do. I had a rough year on account of my daddy had a tough time out there in Ector. He had to put down ten years worth of beef profits and he had to put down the big birds they were pushing for low-fat steaks. It's a red meat, even though it's your big bird, a *ratite*—that means, my daddy says, one of those that can't fly on account of a faulty kind of breastbone and not their weight, the way you might think. And she'd sit right there and hear me talk until I wore my misery out about it. And then she'd be right there, still smiling in that way she had. I always figured that husband of hers to be one granddaddy longlegs of a cold fish, if you ask me."

I was letting my special-ground South American coffee get cold. Had she picked someone my mother would hate on purpose? By instinct? Or just to finally have some choice in her own life? "Did you go to the—funeral?" I asked him. Stunned as I was at the time, I wasn't singling out anybody in the crowd, which I remembered being in the hundreds.

"Not on your life." He smacked the heels of his huge hands together for emphasis. "Elly, I hardly got myself out of my pickup where I spent the night crying and getting stone drunk. No way I was going to come back here and show up in a suit to offer my condolences to those people—I'm restraining my language here—who never appreciated her one little bit." He took out a handkerchief and honked a couple of times. "When that plane went down, I thought about driving right past the barricades and plowing into the wreckage. What held me back was, that truck's a tank. I'd of made a drunk fool of myself, which her memory didn't need."

"That must have been awful."

"You don't begin to grasp the half of it, ma'am." By this time his pocket handkerchief was soaked.

"She thought a lot of you." What a dumb, inadequate thing to say. But maybe he got the idea.

"She tell you about the piano?" he asked, blowing his nose again, slapping his NOTREES cap on the table a couple of times.

"I don't believe—"

"What I did, I got her a piano. Baby grand. Kind of a getting-together present, an engagement present, you could say."

"Did she know?" That was the very last thing in the world I would have expected.

"She was coming out to see it." He honked again.

"She never talked to me about playing anymore. I thought she'd quit."

"I sort of tricked her into it, as a matter of fact." He looked proud. "I went down to Austin High School to see her high school yearbook. More'n likely you can get a look at everything like that you ever wanted to see on the Internet, so they tell me, but I like to heft the real thing, if you understand me, Elly. So I went down there to that big school and they were very obliging. I didn't know the exact years, but I had a rough idea because of knowing her age, and, sure enough, there was this class photo of Terry Hopkins, pretty as you can imagine in a ponytail, looking like this kid, and it said *Piano* and *Tennis* under her interests. Then, the next year, her junior year, look out, Moses, there she was, blossomed into strictly your beauty-queen type, and it didn't say piano anymore, it just said tennis. I asked her about that, when we had a little time together, on that trip over your way it was, and she admitted she used to play a lot, but she quit. So I asked her, would she play something for me sometime? If she had a piano?"

I'd been tearing my warm donut into little crumbs and tossing them on the wooden deck for the sparrows and starlings. The young mothers in shorts and tennies that I remembered from my morning here with Terrell must have all been out of town on the Texas coast or in the Rockies or on some island off Maine, the same as my clients back home. By this time, my cold coffee tasted like what the plumber had got out of my tenant's stopped-up sink in the duplex. I couldn't think straight.

Now it was my turn to borrow the wet, snotty handkerchief. I'd already soaked my paper napkin. "A *piano*," I said, and really broke down.

What more could a guy give you than the chance to start over again and get it right?

20

Heading away from Central Market, past browning Central Park, down Lamar Boulevard, and then out East Sixth Street, I was amazed at how quickly I reached Cisco's, the Mexican bakery where I was meeting Red. I nearly drove past it. Why, it seemed practically downtown, Austin now stretching miles past it. When I was in school, it seemed a big, somewhat daring deal to go way out Sixth Street in the heart of East Austin to eat at Cisco's and watch all the Anglo politicians who came to press the flesh of their Spanish-speaking *compadres*. On a Saturday or Sunday morning, we'd crowd at a table in the back room, pigging out on huevos rancheros, hot biscuits, chorizo, tortillas, sweet pastries. It had seemed almost like going across the border in Laredo.

Today, I passed by the neighborhood regulars in the front room and headed into the packed back room, tables jammed so close together you could hear half a dozen con-versations at once. Although the female waiters still bal-anced those immense platters of the same wonderful food, the crowd had changed. They all looked a lot like Red: pen-cil pushers with short hair. Techno prols in shorts and faded T-shirts, most of them male, most of them half my age, most of them non-Anglo, most of them with cell phones. What feet I could see—making my way through the crunch to where Red sat at a table for two on the side wall—wore Birkenstocks, Tevas, tennies. Not a politician in sight, though the same owner I remembered from a quarter of a century ago still worked the room, shaking every hand.

Red stood, and pulled out my chair. "I got here early," he said.

I had to collect myself a bit when I sat down, from just being with him, and from realizing that this was the first time we'd been out alone together since the Pink Cafe. If you could call being in a room with sixty-odd eating, talking techies alone.

"I saw him," I said. And it came to me that my eyes were probably still red and gummy, and that he could read everything he wanted to know from that.

"Are you okay?"

"I think."

"Why don't we eat first?"

"This is mine; I invited you."

He hesitated a moment, then said, "Fair enough."

In reflex, I touched the wallet in my back pocket. Not to worry: we'd eat on the money I'd been saving for a tank of gas for the trip home, thanks to Daddy's Mobil card. Not bothering with the large menu, I made myself feel better by ordering old favorites: the over-easy huevos rancheros with sausage patties, the tortillas and the hot buttermilk biscuits with strawberry jam. A cup of coffee, which, when it came, tasted, yes, just like plain old hot fresh-out-of-the-Folgerscan coffee. Recovering somewhat with the aid of the pepper-hot salsa, I considered how prudent I'd been at Central Market, to shred my designer donut for the birds and let my designer coffee grow cold, and save myself for serious sustenance.

Red got the chorizo with tortillas. He waited as if he had all the time in the world to hear about Mr. Emu, but his face looked strained. He was forty-seven, if I remembered right, passing for fifty this August morning at eleven o'clock.

"I felt bad," he said, "pressuring you into calling him. Mostly bad because I couldn't seem to let it go. What does it matter now? I kept asking myself. As far as that goes, what did it matter then? But I couldn't get her going to see him out of my mind."

"It's hard," I agreed, "to let someone go, even if they're gone. Because you had something once, you think that gives you a claim." I remembered the talk I'd had with Mayfair, now that we were getting friendly. How possessive we are, she'd said, about everybody going and coming. It all starts with our mamas and daddies, she said. Then, we thought they belonged to us; now, they think we belong to them.

"You talking about Buddy?"

"Mostly." I could remember tearing my hair out when he started wandering, wanting to tear out his. Not able to believe it, after we'd been such hot stuff. Red must have felt that way, too, about my sister.

"What about the guy who sells houses? Birdie's pal?"

"Karl?" I must have blushed. Still, it was okay for him to ask. "He wasn't too happy when 'Uncle Rufus' came to town, I have to say." I smiled, recalling. "But we were never headed for anything more. He's scared of becoming his dad, of getting trapped——"

He ate a few bites of his sausage-scrambled eggs. "For a while I was seeing the Chinese woman from Dell who's helping me out—not much older than my boys. But she said we should stop; she wanted to work with the project, that was something she couldn't get just anywhere. And I wanted her on it."

How easy all this was to talk to Red about, who we'd been having sex with. But then we'd always talked about personal things we couldn't tell anyone else, back there in his old law student's car.

While we let this settle in, we drank our coffee and listened to the exchange at other tables, the big center ones seating eight, family style. Most of the buzz concerned breaking news about Dell, Compaq, smaller companies I didn't know. We heard this one loud guy in a logo-tee on a cell phone, standing in the corner, his back to the room, say, "Can I give you a credit card? Huh? I forgot to pay for the tune-up." And proceed to rattle off his name and his Amex number for anyone in the room to have written down. No one even looked around.

"A different bunch here from the old days," I offered. Wondering, how did they keep the fried eggs so hot yet still runny under the blistering salsa?

"It's packed like this now any hour of the day," Red said. "Late afternoon, there must be a hundred people in here, a lot standing against the wall, talking on the phone or reading the paper, or just having a beer. These kids seem to be at home in crowds."

I ate one of the spicy flat crisp-edged sausages and washed it down. I hadn't really got my mind off Skip Rowland. Think about having a guy so much in love with you he went to your high school and dug out your old class pictures. Terrell had said: "He makes me feel so young." But I hadn't known what she meant. "All right," I said to Red, "how do you want to do this?"

He pushed his wire-rims on top of his head and rubbed his hazel eyes. "However you want."

I began. "I met him at Central Market. You know Central Market?"

He nodded. "Terrell did all her shopping there."

"That's how come I knew it. I'd met her there on the trip for Mother's birthday, five years ago. Big public place." I looked to see if he understood.

"Good idea." A muscle was moving in his jaw.

I got to the basics. He didn't need to know about the NOTREES cap, about the Buddy Marshall resemblance. He didn't need to hear anything that would force him to *see* the guy, sitting there with me. "He knew about the crash. I gathered he was—waiting out there, for the plane." I gave him time to ask something, but he sat still. "He didn't come to the funeral." I thought a minute, then smiled and added, "He didn't want to put on a suit."

Red smiled back, with effort, no doubt understanding that I'd left a lot unsaid.

"He scarcely mentioned his wife; if he knew you'd moved

out he didn't say." The busy waiter swooped up my plate and side dishes, and it wasn't the time to stop her and ask her to leave the tortillas for me to chew on.

"This can't be easy for you," Red allowed.

"Not for any of us," I conceded.

The guy who'd given out his Amex number to the room at large had pulled up a chair at a table for two, now seating four, all heads bent over someone drawing a diagram.

I reapplied my chewed-off copper lipstick, and took a sizeable breath. "He called her *Terry*." I tried to give Red time to deal with that.

He flushed but said nothing. He tasted his coffee.

Then there wasn't much else to hedge about, beat around the bush about. "He bought her a piano." I said it straight out, looking at him.

"He what?" The color left his face, and he sat silently hunched over, as if he'd sustained a blow.

"A baby grand."

He cleaned his glasses and put them on. "Did she know?"

I nodded. "She was going out there to see it."

What could be worse? Your wife fucked someone else, well, in this case, you were moving out anyway, she was pissed you were leaving the cushy job, maybe, or maybe the other guy had buckets of new oil money or old cattle money. Maybe his spread went back to the first land grants, maybe to Santa Anna. Maybe he got off to rustling a civil lawyer's wife. But if he called her by her girlhood name, if he gave her a gift of what had been the most important thing in the world to her back then, how could you deal with that?

Not well, I judged, from the looks of him. I'd finished off

Skip's handkerchief and had none of my own to offer. Red cleaned his glasses again, blinking and looking away.

At least with Buddy, I had got some closure. For one thing, he took up with a woman loaded not only with a paid-up yacht but with a clutch of offshore leases as well. That's whose boat he was steering in that last shot of him with the black wraparound shades. Loud, rich, older. I could deal with that. What had made me wiggy in the extreme was finding out she had *children.* "You gave her kids," I screamed at him the last time I saw him. "I don't mind that you're eating foie gras and soft-shelled crabs and I'm scraping by here on scrambled eggs, trying to learn enough about what grows in pots to fake myself a career. I can live with that. It could be worse: I could be holed up in my old room at Mother's. And I don't even care anymore that you never kept your pecker in your pants, not from hardly day one, all right, day one hundred, one thousand. But you could have given me a kid at least." "They were already hers," he said, fishing up his shirtsleeve for a cigarette. "Same dude who bought her the boats. The same old guy who hung around a dozen years trying to get his hands on those drilling ventures." "I don't care; she's got kids. You've got kids now." "You want a kid, we can walk right through that door and make one on the spot." He'd nodded in the direction of the lone bedroom of my then one-bedroom apartment. He thought he was calling my bluff. But I called his, reasoning I might never again be (a) in his vicinity, (b) off the Pill, and (c) young enough. He nearly came back, he told me later on the phone, when he heard he'd actually pulled off the job.

Red handed me his napkin. It seemed my eyes had filled

up again. For all of them. For Skip Rowland, in his skintight T-shirt through which you could watch his heart trying not to break. For Terrell, making the marriage she was supposed to make, making the children, doing the big house. Finding love, and flying toward it. Mostly for my old friend, who had no way to handle the idea of somebody else knowing to give his estranged wife what he never even knew she wanted: a baby grand piano.

"What will he do with it?" Red asked.

"He didn't say." My feeling was Skip might have wanted to beat it to death with a hammer, but I didn't suggest that.

"She swore to me she never wanted to play another note. At Christmas, at your folks' house—"

"I know, she told me that, too. That she hated playing on demand, those Christmas carols for Mother." (I could see again the young Terrell practicing her first recital piece. Hear Mother come into the living room and interrupt: "You're going to ruin your posture, dear, bending over the keys that way. Why not take a little break?" I could hear Terrell, the last time I came home, before we went out for coffee, "I saw your girl at the piano, does she play? I never think about it anymore, except when Mother makes me. You get over those things you think you can't live without. Is she interested in music? My boys are such jocks, though. I'm proud of that, I have to say, and getting them out on the boat and the tennis courts is, I guess, my contribution, because all the brains come straight from Rufus.")

"You gave him a chance to talk to someone." Red's voice sounded ragged.

"Yes. That's what we wanted to do, wasn't it? To give him

a hearing?" I shivered. The air-conditioning was running so cold I actually had goose bumps on my bare legs, although that might have been a sign of shock. I paid the waiter, giving her an extra something for not rushing us from the table. Every chair in that back room was taken, people scrunched together, calling for more coffee, getting a number off their beepers, telling techie jokes. After what seemed a river of time, I asked, "What do we do now?"

Red seemed to shake himself. He pushed back his chair, looked around as if to get oriented. "I want you to come home with me," he said.

My heart lifted.

"I have something to show you."

21

Following Red's new Nissan in my old Chevy, caravan style to his house in Pflugerville, late that baking August morning, my mind was no longer on Mr. Emu. I had done that, made that very difficult contact. Now my thoughts turned to us, Red and me. I remembered coming here the last time, how I had kissed him, how we had drawn apart. I remembered us sitting on that wide sofa in the large barefloored living room, the children two rooms away, talking of us.

This time, he'd made clear, we would be alone. Taking care to let me know that his computer crew had gone to their main jobs, would not be there moonlighting for him, that his boys were out gathering essentials for Borden's move to New Haven.

Parking, going up the flagstone path under the gray-green live oaks, my chest felt tight, my head light. He led me into the big front room where once his mom and dad must have slept. "Shut your eyes," he said. Then, "Open them."

And, sure enough, he did have something to show me. Every screen had rolling oranges in bright variations, turning round and round like globes. And, on the wall to our

left, where before he'd had a blowup of workers at computers, he now had a world map with orange pins indicating the
gross national production in order: Brazil, the U.S., Spain,
Mexico, Italy, China, Egypt. And, below that, a wide banner
reading, WHERE ARE THE ORANGES?

"Red, how fantastic!" And it was.

"Welcome to oranges dot com." He began to talk of the
contacts they were making with the different countries, of
what they'd sent out from Texas.

As he talked, I tried to imagine WHERE ARE THE OR-
ANGES? going around the globe (an orange with the conti-
nents superimposed) in every tongue. Drawing on my very
pidgin use of two: *Où sont les oranges? ¿Dónde están las naranjas?* Trying to imagine a vertical row of pen-brushed Chinese
characters. The languages of Egypt, India, Indonesia.

Everywhere, he had filled pottery bowls with oranges,
oranges in shapes and shades I'd never seen before. Smooth
skins, pebbly skins, pocked skins, nearly red to deep orange
to almost green; round, oval, pear-shaped, apple-shaped.
Wondrous. Only one thing was missing: the smell of the
fruit. I fished out my key chain, and opening the small Swiss
Army knife I carried for snipping off rose leaves (or thorns),
and selecting an orange with a thick rind, I began to peel it
in a counterclockwise direction. My fingers stinging a little
as the oil was released. I passed a strip of peel to Red, scor-
ing it slightly for a stronger scent (the way you could do
with green pecan husks, making a sudden incense). I tore at
the sections, feeding one to him, and as I licked the juice
from my fingers, the taste of orange filled my mouth, and I
thought of us again.

"It's magic," I told him, watching the six varieties of orange scroll on the screens.

"You can take credit. When you asked, 'Where are the oranges?' that got me to rethink our approach. To ask myself, ourselves: Who tends the trees? The first step was to stop thinking in terms of *worker,* a class word, and to start thinking in terms of citrus *gardener.* First, I looked up the term for someone who grows roses—"

"Rosarian."

"Then I looked up the comparable term for someone who grows and develops new varieties of fruit."

I shook my head. I had no idea.

"Pomologist."

"Apple lover?" I laughed aloud, drawing on my rusty French.

"Fruit lover." He stood leaning against the counter, arms crossed, looking happy. "That opened up the whole thing for us. Once we got off talking about workers' problems and started talking about the concerns of the orange grower, we opened up the conversation to research developments, to climate management. The guy who bred the new navel orange that has the slight taste of both a mango and a papaya, you don't call him a *worker.* You call him a *pomologist.* Hell"—he waved a hand around the room—"a *naturalist.*"

"Yes," I agreed, pleased at his excitement.

He pulled two computer chairs together. "Come sit, Ella. I have something I want to run by you."

All at once I had a sinking feeling. Was all this, the show of oranges, just a way to bring up another matter having to do with my sister? Was I again, as at the Pink Cafe, as back in his law-school car, thinking something was going on between us when it wasn't? "What?" I asked, wary, watching the orange spheres roll on and off the screens. Where moments before it had seemed erotic licking the dripping juice from my fingers, now they merely felt sticky.

"What would you think," Red began, "about writing a letter for us, the way you wrote about that pink house in Old Metairie and those antique roses to Terrell and your mother?"

"My pretend house and garden." I felt embarrassed.

"You made that real, believable. I'd like you to write a newsletter we can put on the Web, the science and practice of fruit culture, the different trees, their care, the dangers, what research is going on. Sort of a letter-to-your-mother on a larger scale."

"*Dear Mother, Dear Mother,* Past the birdbath on a cleared slope, I have planted six orange trees—"

"A Marrs." He smiled. "A low-acid navel bud sport unknown outside Texas."

"A Marrs." I pretended to be writing.

"A Parson Brown. Grown from a seedling that made its way from China to a Florida grove."

"Oh, yes, a Parson Brown."

"A Hamlin, a Pineapple, a Valencia."

Trying to get my mind around the idea, I peeled another orange, this one sweeter, less acidic, and draped the curling rind around my neck, a fragrant citrus lei. How strange: the very idea of being rewarded for my deceitful letters home, creating that cottage in the old, dear part of our parish, with a magnolia in the yard, inventing the garden with the stone wall, the blooms that I transplanted from Belle Vue to my imagined beds.

Red took my hand and pretended to write across my palm. "The freezing point of oranges is twenty-eight degrees. Some groves in Florida and some orchards in the Rio Grande Valley of Texas try spraying the trees with water all night in freezing weather, because freezing releases heat and so it never gets below thirty-two degrees. On the other hand, they say, if you wait too long, the weight of the ice destroys the trees."

Dear Orange Gardener, Dear Orange Gardener. I was greedy for information. How much you had to know, to pass on even the smallest mention. "And—?" Light-headed from his touch, the flavor of the last orange lingering on my tongue, I wanted more.

He tugged a bit at my hair, wrapping it lightly around his hand (something Buddy used to do). "Fruit breathes," he explained. "All fruit breathes, my researchers say. If you want to un-green oranges, you put them in a room with bananas or apples, and those breathe them into full color."

"I don't know about doing your letter," I told him. "I've had enough of making things up."

"We could ship you an orange crate full of books." To demonstrate, he got up and piled a stack of paperbacks, all with oranges on their covers, smooth and glossy, into my arms.

"Do you have catalogues?" I asked. "I love catalogues." The idea was appealing. New plants to learn about. Redolent. Remontant? (Did fruit trees bear more than once a year?)

With histories, genealogies. I grew thrilled with the notion that every single growing thing in the world had such a past.

"We can send catalogues." Red let his hand slip down my arm to the wrist. "You could work on it from Metairie."

"Maybe you ought to find a Henry of Orange," I countered. "Someone who already knows the way of the trees, their blooms and fruits."

"I want Ella," he said, standing close to me, reading my face, "the lover of roses."

"Am I to become also a lover of oranges, then?" I let him put his arms around me, wanting to taste the fruit on his lips.

"Don't you see?" he urged. "It's a way we can work together, a way we can keep in touch. A way for us to see each other that has *nothing at all* to do with family."

"Are you sure?" I asked him, a near whisper at his ear.

"I'm sure about that, and I'm sure about this."

22

He took my hand and led me into his large, fairly bare room—a bed, dresser, old cane-seated rocker, small oak desk and chair. "This was mine," he explained, "growing up." (Which accounted for his setting up the workplace in the front room: no one wanted to sleep in what had once been the parents' bedroom.)

I felt terrified, I had to say. "I have to say I'm terrified," I told him. "Like really scared. I know you too well; I don't know you well enough." I hadn't the words for it, the knowledge that he and I were going to be something different to each other, and so maybe couldn't go back again to what we had been.

Red pulled the thick white curtains and locked the door. "I'm scared, too," he said, his voice low. "I'm scared it'll go wrong and we'll pretend this never happened. A one-time aberration."

"We won't pretend."

He took off his shoes, and I took off mine. Sandals which I placed beside my keys and sunglasses.

I got under the covers of the bed, still in my black tee and best watering shorts, and held the sheet and white spread for him to crawl under, too. "The thing is," I said, "when you start out having sex you're young and dumb and eager and you neck until you think you'll go brain-dead and then when he finally gets it in there—I don't know how it is for the guy—it's such a relief because, hey, you did it." I wriggled out of my shorts and unbuckled his belt. Which gave me such a rush I almost forgot to breathe. "Could you make love to a mutt like me?" I asked, pulling off my skimpy white cotton panties.

"You remember that?" He pulled me so tight against him I could feel his appendix scar.

"I remember a lot," I told him, "but I'm forgetting a lot, too." I let my hands get him out of his shorts, taking the big step, feeling him. "Say my name," I croaked in his ear.

And he did. "Ella," he said, straight out and loud, so I'd know (and he'd know) exactly who he was opening up with his fingers. "I wanted you in the car in the rain in Old Metairie."

"I wanted to stay when we had that great barbeque supper here. Unplug the coffee, wind up the kids, turn off the fruit pickers, and climb into bed."

It felt as if everything that was happening had happened every day for years: making love to Red, my old friend Red, and it wasn't like in the movies, lots of shrieking and clothes tearing. I didn't reach out and grab the headboard, moaning. We weren't pressed together, wild, adulterous, in some seaside summerhouse. I just wanted it until I thought I'd go out of my mind, and took it, and he did, and then, after, we sort of collapsed, still under the covers. Like lovers in the daylight, still shy and breathing hard.

"Was that incest?" I asked him.

He shook his head. "You're not the kid sister anymore."

"It still feels clandestine."

"Anything two adults with children do feels clandestine."

"Because it is——" I had to laugh, looking at it that way.

"Do you need to call home——?" He might have been talking to a sixteen-year-old.

"Just stay here a bit. In bed, if you're sure we have time. Tell me about when you were a kid here. Tell me about the boy whose mother wouldn't call him 'Rufus.' Something from then, before, you know, you showed up at our yellow frame house on the bluff above the creek."

We lay on our backs, heads propped on pillows. He had his hand on my stomach, but you never feel your stomach is flat enough and I didn't want it any higher, because you never feel your tits are big enough, so I slid it down to my thigh, where it felt comfortable.

"I liked my dad," he said, "despite the fact he never got his act together. He joked around, though a lot of the time what he found funny was at someone else's expense. My mom took his failures hard."

"I didn't know any of that, at first, about your family, not when you first started coming around, anyway. My daddy would say, 'An up-and-coming young man.' Mother would say, 'Such a nice young man with a nice future.' I guess, come to think of it, they still say that——" Because he was who he'd always been.

"You have no idea, Ella," he told me, leaning up on one elbow, "what it did for me, being welcome at your parents' house; what being approved of by them meant. I suppose from the start, I was marrying your family as much as I was marrying Terrell. She must have sensed that. That must have been part of the trouble."

"You wanted in and I wanted out."

He traced my collarbone. "When I waded through that backyard swamp and knocked on that screen door with the rip in it big enough for a mosquito the size of a crawdad to crawl through, and that daughter of yours asked me, 'Would you like a peanut butter sandwich, Uncle Rufus,' I was ready to move in. I felt I'd come home."

I kissed his nose, feeling a little response down below. I kissed it again. "I liked you back then, when you were a student."

"I was trying to impress you." He found my stomach again, and above and below, but just a hello, because his hands didn't know me yet.

I rolled over and looked at him, at his suntanned face, his hazel eyes, his too-short graying dark hair. Having an attack of fear-of-loss, I asked, "Can we keep this?"

He hesitated. "I don't know. I worry you'll get home to Metairie and go back to your roses and that slick guy who takes you to the movies on Saturday. And this will seem— too far away, too complicated."

"I won't forget. Your name is Rufus, that's Red to me and your mom."

After a pause, he said, "You were talking earlier about the first time you did it, in a car—"

"Come on, hey. I was just trying to say that when you've had sex for so many years with somebody—and then when you're with somebody that you, that matters—I was trying to say it gets awkward. The first time, you're just glad to—do it."

"Was that the first time for you, with Buddy?"

"I should think." I laughed and shook my head at that ancient time. "He got me in high school. If I hadn't run away when I did, Mother would have kicked me out. I know she thought I was preggers, but I wasn't."

"Terrell and I waited a long time, I guess you know, such a long time, till she got her ring. I thought it had to do with her needing to feel she'd held out for marriage. But then—" His voice faltered a bit, and he sat up against the white pillows. "It turned out I wasn't the first."

"She *told* you that?" I lay flat back, burrowing my head against his shoulder, amazed.

"It shouldn't have mattered. I'd . . . been with a girl in high school myself. But it got under my skin. She called it a double standard. But it was that she made such a big deal out of waiting."

How could I not know about this? Though what Terrell did in that regard, once she got on the university campus, was naturally not my business. Except she'd liked confiding. Way before Mr. Emu. "Oh, Red," I said, "that had to do with Mother. Marrying from home in a proper formal church wedding, saving herself, all that."

"I never pressed her." He slipped a hand into my hair.

I couldn't help it, knowledge stirred in my midsection. And I knew as sharply as if I'd been run through with a knife, that of course she had fucked someone else first, and of course it had been Buddy. Twisting upright, as if from a blade, I thought back to the way, every time I'd seen her or talked to her on the phone, she'd asked me, What do you hear from Buddy? Do you ever hear from Buddy? Do you still miss Buddy? And could hear again the way her voice would change, just that little barely noticeable bit. I shut my eyes and tried to hear her again. The first time she told me about Mr. Emu, her saying, "I never had what you had with Buddy." But now I heard it as "I never had *with Buddy* what you had." I heard her telling me without telling me. Her confession. How could it have been an accident: the rancher from Notrees his spitting image?

I tried to remember what Buddy used to say about her, back when we'd first started hanging out, when he'd been getting in my pants in the car, when he was driving me wild with finding out what my body was all about. "You're a lot hotter than your sis," he said. "You've got it all over her, El," he said. I thought he meant, of course I thought he meant, that he was laying out the reason he'd stopped hanging around her and taken up with me: we made the seas part and lit the sky with fire. It never dawned on me, of course it didn't, that he meant he'd *been there first*. But he had. And they did. And naturally she had to break it up, no way she could have so much as had a public beer with someone who had no future. Not at our mother's house.

Pushing away Red's hand, I jumped out of bed, hunting around on the floor for my panties. "Did you set me up for that? Waiting till after we'd done it?"

He stood also, not starting to dress. "What are you talking about? Ella, what did I say?"

"You know it was Buddy she screwed first. You know that." Tears streaked my cheeks.

He took a step back; then, his face gone white, he reached for his shorts. "I don't know that."

I was shouting. "You think I don't realize I've always been second choice to everyone? First to my parents, then to my randy dumb lying husband, now to you? You think I don't understand that you only ever wanted me because I'm *her sister,* the one who knows about Mr. Emu and the airplane and the piano, and who she really was back then, and Buddy. You think I don't know that as long as you're screwing me, you've *still got her?*"

He reached for my shoulders. "Ella, listen to me."

But instead we heard the sound of the boys' car squealing into the driveway, and were barely at the coffeepot when they came, laden with packages, bursting through the door.

23

I came in from Red's, my body still dazed from lovemaking, my heart still scored, sore, from our fight, to find Daddy and Birdie unloading sacks of groceries. My daughter's eyes big as saucers, presumably at the unthrifty nature of her granddad. Daddy, flapping his shirttail and downing a full glass of water without ice, keeping up his swallowing, announced that they had passed the mail carrier in shorts and a pith helmet, looking like a heatstroke about to happen.

I knew this would allow him to embark on one of his favorite discourses: a complete history of the postal service beginning with the first adhesive stamp sold for prepayment of postage before the Civil War. "I'm going to set the record straight for this girlie, here," he told me as I edged toward the door. "I bet your fine daughter did not know that the familiar slogan 'Neither snow, nor rain, nor heat, nor gloom of night shall stay these couriers from the swift completion of their appointed rounds' did not originally refer to the postal service but to the mounted messengers of King Xerxes of Persia."

She did not.

Shaky, feeling that I might jump out of my skin, I kissed

them both and beat a retreat up the stairs. Climbing, I could hear him on the early horse-and-buggy days of Rural Free Delivery.

In the old room, I stretched out on the bed that had been mine a few light-years ago, my head facing north, my arms east and west. (I used to have to imagine myself in bed in this room to get a bearing on direction. And still sometimes felt that, wherever I was, the sun should be rising over my left shoulder, setting over my right.) It was a mistake and I knew it, to lie here, a pillow over my head, Mother's monogram stitched above my nose, still stung to numbness by the idea of my sister with Buddy.

I didn't want to mess up what had been so special—the oranges, Red's arms in bed, the idea that we could truly be getting something started between us. But nonetheless and notwithstanding, I felt sick to my stomach. Wondering if Terrell might indeed have been happier if she'd been the one who'd run off with Buddy. Trying to picture her in that mega-fancy repo yacht he'd sent photos of, her sunshades on, hair streaked a lemon blond by the Gulf Coast sun, her arm draped around his bare shoulder, a big grin on her tanned face. Maybe waving at the camera: So long, bye-bye.

I could see, a quarter of a century ago, Mother's flowered living room, see Daddy through the open doorway of his library. See Mother, trim and not much older than I was now, scoot down the hall to answer the door, calling out, "Why, come in, Rufus." Leading him into the chintzy living room, her voice rising, "Terrell, dear, your young man is here—"

Could see him, the guy my mom had got all aflutter

about, the one my daddy, the towering, bearded young professor, was rising to greet, hand outstretched. The lean law
student in horn-rim glasses with the mop of curly dark hair,
come to court their elder daughter.

What I saw now, pulled from memory like a forgotten
snapshot, what I had not wanted to see then, so infatuated
was I already with Buddy, was the two of them, standing
close enough to touch, in the living room the moment
before the doorbell rang: my sister and Buddy Marshall.
Looking, the pair, like every school's Homecoming Queen
and King, him big, totally gorgeous, those blue eyes, that
kind of girl-melting grin, her tall, with honey hair, that
Texas tan, long legs in short pink shorts—gazing up at him.

Saw how he stepped back, glowering, when Red came in.

Saw how she shrugged and looked from him to Mother.

"Rufus," Mother had said, "I'm sure you've met our other
daughter, Ella. And her friend here—" She frowned at
Buddy. "I'm sorry—you boys and your nicknames."

"It's Buddy, ma'am, and that's my *name.*"

What I'd remembered, all I'd wanted to remember, was
the way he'd come over to my side, the way the touch of his
hand on my arm had sent goose bumps to my hairline.

I groaned and pressed my face into the musty pillow in its
laundered case. I'd always been second choice to everyone.
Each of them, the lot of them, thinking: Oh, yes, Ella. All
we've got left is Ella.

Birdie knocked on the door. "Mom?"

She was in her baggy shorts and tank top, hair loose, face
scrubbed. "Did you have a date with Uncle Rufus this morning?" she asked.

"Yes, I did. We had breakfast at a Mexican cafe and then I saw a wonderful room full of oranges."

"Is that why you're crying?"

"Am I?" I tested my wet face, finding evidence she was right. "That's silly, isn't it?"

"No, that's what girls do. I and Felice have friends who do that. The ones who work at the Pink Mall? They have a date and then they cry a lot." She hesitated. "Did you used to do that with my daddy?"

"I did," I admitted, a more than fair statement. And that allowed me to locate a weak smile. Her wanting to think that Uncle Rufus didn't have anything over her daddy. "What do boys do?" I asked her, trying to pull myself together. "After they've had a date?" And, truthfully, I did wonder what Red was doing over there, in that house of his, after everything we'd done and said, the good parts and the bad.

"They kick things, that's what our friends say. They kick things with other guys, balls or something. Soccer players, they date all the time."

This cheered me no small bit. Imagining Red giving a field-goal heft to the pillow left on the floor by his bed, to the rolled-up pair of socks he'd had on. Even, perhaps, angry, to the half-eaten orange left in the pottery bowl in the computer room. Bare foot smacking orange rind.

"Birdie, are you up there?" A man's voice called to her up the stairs.

"Hello, Uncle Rufus," my daughter blared back. "I and my mom will be down in a minute."

I sat on the side of the bed and put on my sandals, then stood and peered into the dresser mirror. Did I still look as if I'd just come from his bed? Were my feelings all over my face?

"After you have a date with Karl, he always kids with me about that head cheerleader he made up," Birdie said. "I think men want you to know that they aren't taking your mom away from you, that they aren't trouble. Like maybe Uncle Rufus is here to kid with me?"

"You're good with pattern recognition," I told my daughter, making a wide smile so she'd know this was some kind of grown-up joke. "That'll come in handy."

She hesitated. "Do you like Uncle Rufus better than Karl?"

"I guess I do." I didn't see any point in explaining all the gray areas involved in the adult man-woman thing. Anyway, it might be she saw things clearer than I did. "What do you think?"

"Karl isn't a daddy," she said, frowning with trying to say it right, "so he doesn't know a lot of things that daddies know. That I bet even my daddy knew."

How could I have caviled about who Buddy stuck it in and when? I was the one who got this daughter. For that, I had never taken his name in vain, or hardly ever, and felt ashamed of having done so in the deep hurt of my mind. "He did," I told her, with surety and warmth. "Your daddy wasn't much for settling down with anybody, he hadn't seen that as being very helpful to his own daddy, but he did what he said he would do, and he knew the very best thing he ever did in his life was you." For one who'd lied to most everyone in her time, this one stuck a bit in my throat. But who knew? Maybe it was true. Maybe it was.

"I guess I better go see Uncle Rufus," Birdie said, looking happy at my answer. "So he'll know I'm not mad at him because you had a date with him."

¿Dónde están las naranjas? Où sont les oranges? Where are the oranges? Dear Gardener, Dear Gardener, help me out here. Floods, droughts, freezes, heat waves, fights between lovers, all those variables of temperature and moisture. How could you ever be sure your tree would bear fruit?

24

All of them were in the library when I came down, shod and brushed, Red and his boys, Daddy, Birdie. All except Mother, who, my daddy said, had gone to get her hair done. He'd taken her and would pick her up. "Salon matters are out of my bailiwick," he said, meaning, no doubt, that his health letters were short on reports about the efficacy of a good cut and color.

Red held out his hand. "Did you get any lunch?" he asked. "I'm afraid we took too long looking up the options of my citrus growers."

"We ate so much at Cisco's—I wasn't hungry anymore." It felt more awkward even than I imagined, with the boys staring at us, the fight unsettled between us.

We'd stood in his kitchen, clothes barely back on, scarcely an hour ago, looking at the perk pot and one another as if at foreign objects. Then Red (easily it seemed to me), told his sons, "Ella came by to see my fancy orange display. But she stuck around long enough for us to have a fight." To which they'd said, "Hi, Dad," and "Hi, Aunt Ella," looking at the walls, then, when we went about the business of getting our mugs, they seemed to relax. They spread out their considerable Yalie purchases for us to admire. Their general attitude conveying: Adults, you figure them out.

When Red walked me to my car, I had to admit that what he'd told them had worked well. At least it took their minds off the obvious conclusion they could come to looking at our kiss-smeared faces, our general disarray. That we'd just had sex. Although, I would have bet, at that moment they might have been bird-dogging around his room, seeing the sheets half on the floor, taking in the smell.

"Good for them to find out fights don't mean the world ends," he had said.

"Don't they?" I burned half the remaining rubber on my tires taking my hurt feelings out of Pflugerville.

"Mom?" Birdie tugged on my tee, her face glowing, "Uncle Rufus says he wants to buy me a cello so I can play like *this*—" She held up the Brahms Double Concerto for Violin and Cello in A minor. "But I told him he didn't have to buy me a cello just because he had a date this morning with my mom."

"Sheeesh," Bailey said, looking skyward, scooting down in the chair until he all but sat on his shoulders, his body language asking: How come it had been his lot to be born into this family?

"Birdie—" Borden leaned forward, his elbows on his thighs, sitting the way his dad often did, his one-stripe polo tee tucked in, his brow furrowed with the effort to explain matters. "You don't have to say everything you think."

"It's all right if you don't do that, Borden," Birdie came back at him, "because you're going to Yale. But it's all right if I do."

The library was the one room in Mother's lemon-yellow, leaf-green matched and decorated house that belonged to Daddy. His walnut desk was there, covered with volumes stuck with slips of paper. And stacks of pages of his *History of a Historian* in progress, where it had been since he retired from the University of Texas. As if he could be sure he'd last as long as it and he were still unfinished.

One wall had floor-to-ceiling books, most on the settlement of the Mediterranean Sea, since that was his specialty. But a lot of large gift volumes or sets as well—*The Rise and Fall of the Roman Empire, Lives of the Queens of England, Dutch Settlement in the New World*—because what else do you give a historian for a gift? (Except yellow-striped ties for Father's Day.) The rug was well worn, American Indian, the two leather chairs where the boys sat, old and cracked, a deep persimmon. A framed copy of an early faded map of the Mediterranean hung behind his massive desk.

Red looked at me, and when he spoke his voice sounded raw. "Sometimes," he said, "somebody wants to do something and they don't get around to it in time. My boys and I talked it over, and we decided that Birdie's Aunt Terrell would want some of the money she left us to be used to buy a musical instrument for somebody who really wants it."

Bailey, squirming around, added, "I guess maybe you didn't know my mom played the piano."

"I do know," I told him, choking up.

"Gosh," Birdie said, "that's really nice of you, Uncle Rufus, and you, too, Bailey and Borden, but I couldn't let you do that. On account of my friend Felice, we play together, and she doesn't have the money for her own instrument either, and I couldn't let her be the only one in Junior String Project who has to play a loaner." And she came over and gave Red a big kiss, standing on tiptoe.

"Do you even know what a cello *costs?*" Borden asked, slicking back his preppie hair with a practiced hand. "We're talking about a good one."

Birdie walked over and stopped by her older cousin's chair. "If you mean a really good cello? My teacher who plays in an orchestra, he's the best or nearly the best, his cello costs twenty thousand. But naturally if you are doing the concert-stage-in-Europe kind of playing, which I won't ever be doing, then I guess you can pay five hundred thousand, you know, for one made in 1700 in Italy or like that."

"Well, double duh," Borden said. "Excuse us. We wanted to do something decent for you, in Mom's memory." His face cracked just a bit, having to talk about his mother.

"I know that, Borden," Birdie said, putting one of her firm hands on his shoulder. "But you were being condescending about my cello playing. That's like you're supposed to be real grateful if I was giving you a scholarship to a junior college in North Texas, when what you wanted was to go to Yale. My teacher's fine cello costs less than one year at your good school is going to cost you. And even that eighteenth-century cello, back when they were violoncellos, costs less than your education that lets you go in all directions is going to cost you."

Bailey half rose out of the leather chair in defense of his brother. "Just because you're a squatty girl with hairy legs doesn't mean you know it all."

Red started to move, but I put my hand on his arm, and kept it there.

Sounding angry, he dropped his voice. "How come *they* get to fight—?"

"They're better at it—," I whispered back, sending him a smile, but meaning it, too.

"Ella—" He spoke so low I could barely hear him. "Don't you know I'm doing this for *you?*"

All I could do was nod.

Then he asked Birdie, "What does your friend Felice play?"

"She's a flutist, Uncle Rufus."

"What could you and Felice both get good-condition student instruments for?"

Birdie stood in the middle of the small library, cooling off from getting mad at her cousin. "My teacher says you can get a good learning cello for two thousand and a good mid-line open-hole flute for two thousand. Not your all-silver handmade for eight thousand or one of the best grenadilla-wood flutes, like that, for twenty. That's what he said. That's what Felice and I are saving our money for. We baby-sit and we pet-sit, and we make a lot in the summer. Sometimes we make forty dollars a month."

She looked really proud, my daughter, but I noticed the two boys looking down at their bare tanned knees, sticking out of shorts either pair of which cost more than her month's earnings.

Red got a piece of scrap paper from his pocket and scratched a few figures. "How's this for a proposition,

Birdie—we can come up with three thousand, the boys and I, that's one each, plus I'll pay you forty dollars a day to board and room Bailey the week I drive Borden to New Haven and back. I figure dropping him off with you in Old Metairie on the way will save that much."

I thought my younger nephew was going to have an attack on the spot. He grabbed his head, he threw his arms in the air, he hollered, "Daaaaaad."

Borden broke out in a guffaw. "Dumbo-sitting."

Birdie giggled. "That's more than I get for cats."

Bailey glared at his dad. "Is that what you two were arguing about? Who got stuck with me? Is it?"

I couldn't believe he said it, that he could think such a thing. This kid, worth his weight in treasures. "Naw," I said, before Red could answer. "We were fighting about who got stuck with *me*."

Both boys looked at me funny, then looked at their dad.

"That leaves you seven hundred twenty short," Red told Birdie, showing her his figures. And it really gave me a solid lump in my chest, that he made it a deal; that he didn't just give the girls the whole thing. I knew he was aching for some need for reparation; that two student instruments hardly cost the price of the piano stool on a Steinway baby grand. But, still, he was treating this like a serious, quantifiable transaction.

"We each have a hundred and sixty dollars saved up to buy our instruments. I bet you, Uncle Rufus, that the music stores—I would get mine at a violin store and she would get hers at the orchestra store—could find us one just a little bit not as good."

It was at this point—when the boys were making sight gags to each other, Bailey making an imaginary noose out of his hands, letting his head loll to one side, Borden pretending his fingers were pistols aimed at his brother—that Daddy rose from his seat behind the desk, where he had been so silent we'd all forgotten he was there. "What is this? What's going on? Nobody told me my granddaughter needed a cello." He looked around the history-filled room, a sea yawning in its frame behind him, five surprised faces looking back.

Of course he wasn't only talking about Birdie or Birdie's cello. Any more than Red had been, than the rest of us had been. His face crumpled, and he stood unsteady on his feet, looming over the top of his desk as he said, "She used to play. We liked to hear her play. Your aunt had a lot of talent, Girlie. She took lessons on that piano in there." He gestured with his arm, which stayed fixed in the air, pointing. "We'll sell it now. No need to have that sitting here, a reminder. Something your grandmother, your mother, Ella, something she has to dust every week of her life. We'll sell it. Let the piano buy Birdie her cello." He leaned forward, both hands supporting him. "Let the piano buy Birdie her cello."

The rest of us—Red, the boys, and I—caught up in our own feelings, our own personal guilt, didn't answer. But Birdie, reasonable, told him, "Granddaddy, you can't sell that to anybody, because nobody can play it. Don't you know it's totally out of tune? Didn't Aunt Terrell tell you?" She left the library and went into the living room, calling out, "Listen, Granddaddy." And then in her fullest voice she sang the scale, "Do, re, mi . . ." Each time hitting a key on the piano that sounded flat, dull, so far off the note that each and every one of us could hear it.

"Nobody told me," Daddy said, breaking into a sob. "We thought it was good enough. Nobody ever told me."

"Sheeesh," Bailey groaned, standing and studying the spines of a row of ancient chronicles.

"What'd you have to do that for, Dad?" Borden's voice rose, his face red. "Why'd you have to make a big deal about it? Couldn't you just have paid for the instruments and dropped it?"

Red took my hand, while both his boys found other places to look. His eyes were red. "We sang those Christmas carols and *none of us listened.*"

"This is a wonderful gift you're giving," I told him, no longer having the wish to fight.

25

Daddy, fixing our breakfast, looked as if he might be getting ready for the first day of classes in a new semester. He'd trimmed his beard, tightened the screws in his eyeglasses so they wouldn't slip down his nose, and put on a freshly laundered light blue professor's shirt and his best suit vest and trousers. And had on Sunday shoes instead of his bedroom slippers. If I'd for a moment forgotten that the former student of Mother's was due for a visit this morning, his appearance and demeanor were instant reminders.

Plus, in honor of the occasion, my daughter had pulled her shawl of hair back into a neat thick plait, and had *shaved her legs.* "Granddaddy said today was important to Grandmom," she'd explained when she appeared from the bathroom upstairs, all scrubbed, talking while I ironed my café au lait dress on the bed. "I think he meant he wanted me to look nice."

Yes, *nice.* I, too, had done my best, with barrettes and lipstick, a little color on my cheeks, the pressed dress, pale hose, sandals. Doing what I could to turn myself, turn Ella, into a presentable daughter.

My mind was on Red. We had talked late last night, me

taking the phone around the corner into the large hall closet by the bathroom while Birdie slept, just as Terrell had often done in high school, when we shared a room. We talked mostly about the logistics of Bailey staying with me in Old Metairie, a bit of temporary custody which warmed the region under my ancient cotton nightie. He admitted he'd suggested that on impulse, an impulse having to do with wanting to see me both directions on his drive east.

"It'll get him out of the impasse between my dad's place and all his old buddies in West Lake Hills. Give him time to think over what he wants to do."

"He can help me with the plumber," I suggested, leaning my back against the wall beneath where Terrell's and my clothes had once hung. I'd had a call that afternoon from my tenant, the teacher, about the recent flooding, and had made a raft of promises.

"I'll take you back to dinner at the Pink Cafe. We can start over," he offered.

"You can carry me through the swamp in my backyard again." I shut my eyes thinking of that, wanting him.

"Can I see you tomorrow? Before you go?" His voice sounded slightly muffled, and I wondered if he called from the bedroom, his childhood bedroom, where I'd piled my panties, sandals, and sunglasses on the floor.

"We're leaving at dawn," I told him.

"I love you, Ella."

But I had said, "Not now," gazing, like an idiot, at my watch. "It's too soon or too late or something."

Today, at the breakfast table, the hot fried eggs staring

back at me, I listened to Daddy holding forth on the lack of objectivity on the part of historians in relation to History. In plain words, how he was sick and tired of reading every single day in the newspaper some commentator's explanation of this year's crop-withering, livestock-starving, aquifer-depleting drought. How each and every one took their personal misery about the loss of their cattle and the lack of rain in their watersheds and the parching of their grasslands, and compared it to the disaster nearest his or her own birth—the drought of 1917 (Texas's driest year), the Dust Bowl of the thirties, the arid, choking fifties. Turning it into some universal economic or geographical or even social theory.

Birdie, rapt, attended to every word as a granddaughter should, while Daddy stirred together a fresh-peach coffee cake, with the last of the Hill Country's summer crop, accidentally dropping an egg on the floor, which took a sheaf of paper towels to remedy.

"Tell me the woman's name again," I asked him, pushing my eggs about my plate. A sign of stress: Ella with no appetite.

"Daughter," Daddy said, washing away the last trace of his mess, "that will have to wait a spell. I am not at the peak of my concentration, here. Your mother, I might as well mention, is still evidencing some reluctance to welcome this former student into our home."

"She's not going to stay back in the bedroom, is she?"

He brushed the cake flour off the front of his good suit pants. "I am confident," he said firmly, "that everything will be copacetic once the moment arrives." Looking anything but, he washed up our plates and checked that the oven had heated up.

"What can I do, Granddaddy?" Birdie asked, in her lavender Amish cello-playing dress and the Chinese slippers she'd borrowed from Felice.

"Let me have a spell in the library with your mother," he requested. "You keep an eye on my peach cake here. Twenty minutes ought to do it."

"All right," she said.

In his library, Daddy recalled the visitor's name. "Sadie Grimes. Sadie Clark, she was back then. There were a pair of sisters, that's what her letter reported."

I sat in the persimmon leather chair where yesterday Bailey had gone bananas learning he was to be in my care for a week. My heart still both light and heavy with what had gone on in this room.

"Ella, girl," Daddy began, safely behind the width of his paper-stacked walnut desk. "I think it's time you were put in full possession of matters relating to your mother and me before we were blessed with our fine daughters. Being an historian, I know that there are a lot of factors bearing on any one event. But, it seems to me, with your mother's recent trouble, and with the possible upset today may cause her, I'd be amiss not to put certain information in your hands."

I felt totally lost. "Whatever you want to tell me, Daddy," I said.

"You take these letters. I've saved them long enough. The reason for keeping them a closed subject is moot, with your sister gone." His voice wobbled slightly, then he opened a drawer and pulled out a folder, removing two envelopes and handing them to me, one thin and palest yellow, one thick and a stock white.

"Keep an open mind," he admonished.

May 10, 1950

My dear Judah,

I reread your letter over and over, as I have all of the others. You don't know the happiness your correspondence provides me. I, also, think of our time together on your last visit here daily, and count the days until you can return.

I know our East Texas life seems slow and perhaps not as challenging as your academic life in Austin, but in our way, my way, it has its rewards. I have thrown myself into the work of tending these small children whom fate has placed in my hands. There is a mystery here I mean to solve. The migrant Mexican children, whose fathers work the hay and lumber mills, when they are older, will have access to every grade of the white schools here in town, which the Negro children, most of whose fathers work the oil rigs here, do not. Yet the lack of language seems to me (a mere observer, as teachers of the young are) a handicap more arduous to overcome than the separate schooling of the Negroes, who, after all, share the language of our King James Bible and the mutual language of our grandmothers. It makes my task a heavy one, not being myself a Spanish speaker. Nor am I sure I can make proper headway otherwise to prepare these small eager

*children for our public schools in which they will be, in
another year or two, enrolled.*

*This topic (about which I fear I have gone on too long,
and please forgive me, especially since I write to one who
has the breadth and distance of History at his disposal)
brings me, reluctantly, to your question of last week:Will
I marry you and move to Austin? I cannot, at this
moment in time, say yes with a light heart. I love you
dearly, which I am not ashamed or embarrassed to
confess. But I do believe that it is not my destiny to rear
children of my own, but rather, that my "calling,"if I do
not elevate myself too highly, is here.*

*We will talk more when you come. Please do not give
up on me. Until then, may God look after you.*

> *Your,*
> *Agatha*

AGATHA ADAMS
ANGELINA COUNTY, TEXAS

I looked across at my daddy, as if the answer to the questions raised by this long-ago letter might be on his stricken
face. "Mother? This was from Mother?" I couldn't conceive
of it.

"Read on," he said. "And don't think too harshly of that
young man I was."

December 20, 1950

Dearest Agatha,

*I miss you daily, although I am pleased to think of you
in East Texas, in what must still feel somewhat like*

"home" to you. I trust your mother is pleased with the progress of your pregnancy, and will allow you to come back into my care soon, for it is almost too late in term for you to be traveling.

I confess, I do have my heart set on naming our firstborn Samuel, a strong name, with a good scriptural promise, although I certainly understand your wish to name him for your father, John. (Still, one can see that John Hopkins could possibly be a confusing name, so similar to a fine institution). But let us not even hint of a quarrel. I am not inflexible. Nor would I be anything but glad should we be blessed with a daughter whom you might want to call after some branch of your own family.

And now, my helpmeet and my beloved, I must close. I wish you were here with me. East Texas seems as far away as China. Hurry home.

> Your loving husband,
> Judah

J. HOPKINS
AUSTIN, TEXAS

My first thought was that I had never known these people, that they were unknowable, having ceased to exist. This Agatha, a girl of twenty-two who did not want to be a wife or mother, later making that very persistent husband and those children the center of her life. It broke my heart. And that callow teacher Judah, suffused with pride: a wife, an heir on the way, a Ph.D. in hand. Already lonely. That broke my heart, too.

"Thank you, Daddy," I said, folding the letters, fitting them in the envelopes, and handing them back to him.

"You see the way things were," he said, looking disheartened, forlorn.

Did I? What had I missed? I took the letters back.

"Your mother and I married in July; your sister was born in February."

I had to count on my fingers. I'd paid no attention to the dates on the letters, past seeing they were before we'd been born. That my mother had married, shamed and pregnant, was incomprehensible. My mother? We'd always celebrated their anniversary on Valentine's Day. So romantic. My sister's birthday a year later almost to the day. So perfect. But how could I, in the late nineties, have possibly understood what it meant in 1950 to "have" to marry? For a girl such as Agatha Adams. Or, perhaps, for any girl.

"I didn't know any other way to win your mother," Daddy confessed, his face streaked. "She meant to stay." He studied his desk. "I've had to live with that."

My mother, well before she was anyone's, speaking of her work with the young as her "calling." Asking God to bless the cultured man who'd come courting her. How much guilt she must have felt. I remembered going with Mother and Terrell to the small limestone Episcopal church, more than a century old, in downtown Austin, never missing a Sunday in Advent, never missing a Palm Sunday or an Easter. The words of the sermon—grace, shame, sin, salvation, sacrifice—the lexicon of my mother's faith. And we, sitting on either side of her, her visible good works.

And now, as near as I could tell, she no longer went to

church at all. Her back turned on the Word, on God, after my sister's death.

I couldn't grasp it, this new glimpse into the past. My head and midsection felt turned inside out. "Does this woman—this Mrs. Grimes—know Mother's story?" I asked after a long silence.

Daddy shook his head, mopping his face. "I think not. After nearly fifty years? She was just a slip of a child at the time, Ella. But your mother—" He sighed and put away the letters. "She's got it in her head it was common gossip in the county."

I took his big hands in mine. "It's all right," I told him. "It's all right." And I sat with him like that, silent and sickened by the knowledge of how each generation lied to the next. Saddened at the thought of the lives my sister and I had with such care invented for our mother; saddened to breaking at the realization of the life she had invented for us.

26

The woman at the door, when I opened it, looked very East Texas: gentle smile, flowered summer dress, faint floral scent, patent-leather pumps. Black. She put out her firm hand. "Sadie Grimes. Now you would be——?"

"I'm Agatha's daughter Ella. There were two of us. My sister Terrell died in January."

"We did hear that unfortunate news, yes. But I thank you, lest I say the wrong thing in speaking with your mother." She patted at her damp face with a lace handkerchief.

"Please come in. I'm visiting here from Louisiana with my own daughter."

"How nice for your family."

I led Mrs. Grimes into the cool living room, where Daddy waited with Birdie. Mother had not yet come out of her bedroom, though surely she had heard the doorbell. I made the introductions, trying to mind my manners. "This is my daughter, Birdie, and my daddy, Judah Hopkins. And this is Sadie Grimes."

"That's a fine name, Mr. Hopkins," she said at once. "Judah, one of the sons of Jacob."

"My word," Daddy said, bowing from the waist until his

forehead was even with that of the visitor. "That's a first, someone knowing Bible names in today's world. Did you hear that, Ella?"

"My brother-in-law is named Issachar. You can imagine how that tormented him in school."

"My brother Reuben was a judge in Ector County."

"Certainly, certainly," Mrs. Grimes declared, nodding her head. "My daddy worked out in Ector in the oil fields, then he moved to Angelina County after, taking a job making oil-field pumps, a step up for a man of his opportunities in the 1940s."

Daddy helped her get seated in one of the green armchairs, then eased himself into the other. Birdie and I sat facing each other on the small flowered sofas. No sign of Mother. We all looked at one another.

"You don't find many people interested in those fine old names these days," Daddy said. He was speaking to our guest, but his eyes were on the living room door.

Breaking the strained silence, Birdie attempted to be sociable. "Did you know I play the cello, Mrs. Grimes?"

"Why, no, dear," Sadie Grimes said, "I don't believe I did. My mama was a fine church organist and that talent has passed on down in our family. That's a priceless gift to have."

"I and my friend—" Birdie began.

But then we heard Mother come down the hall, and there she was, composed, her hair a deep auburn, freshly done, in an apricot linen dress with white collar, her single strand of pearls. She smiled at everyone as if the curtain had just opened on her show. "Well, now, you must be Sadie Clark," she said in a rush, giving the rising woman a little squeeze, telling her to please, sit down. "Though I have to say, I wouldn't have known you, all grown up." She made a musical laugh. "That's all so long ago, isn't it?" She sat beside me on the flowered sofa, reaching out a hand to pat my knee. "I'm sure you've met my lovely daughter, Ella. Doesn't she look nice in taupe? So becoming with her chestnut hair."

"It's an honor to see you again," Sadie said, breaking into a generous smile, "and to meet your fine family. Your husband and I were discussing Old Testament names."

"Don't you have something prepared for our guest?" Mother asked Daddy, in the upbeat tone of someone running a children's birthday party.

"Indeed I do," he replied, getting to his feet and lumbering off to the kitchen.

I was having a hard time getting my breath. Mother's hand had stayed on my knee, and after every remark she turned in my direction, beaming on me as if I were a new discovery.

"I have to apologize, Sadie. Ordinarily, I'd have asked you out into the garden, which used to be my pride and joy; although I have never been the gardener my daughter Ella is, still I took pleasure in it. My azaleas did especially well. But not in this devastating weather. Not a drop of rain in a hundred days."

"Our rivers are wanting water," her former student said, looking, for the first time, at a bit of a loss.

Daddy brought in a plate of fresh-peach coffee cake squares, still warm, that he'd dusted with powdered sugar (along with the tops of his shoes). "Now, then," he said. "What would you ladies like to drink?"

"I'd enjoy some iced tea," Sadie suggested, fanning herself with a church fan though the house was quite cool, "if that isn't trouble for you."

"I keep a jar of sun tea in the icebox," Daddy said, for a moment in his anxiety forgetting to say *refrigerator*. "I'm sure that's fine with everyone."

Then Mother launched into a yard story, just as if this were a common occurrence, someone from her past appearing after forty-eight years. "Did you know that squirrels build nests? I had no earthly idea. Here I was, looking out at the ligustrum that brushes against the side of the house, making us think sometimes, when we're in bed, that someone is in the yard. At any rate, there I was, standing on a straight chair peering out our bedroom window, trying to see what that pile of twigs and leaves was in the top of the shrub, expecting to see a robin's egg perhaps, and instead, there was this curled up ball, a common squirrel—"

"I believe I did know that," Sadie offered gamely.

Daddy brought in a tray of iced tea and placed it on the glass-topped coffee table. He had used the inherited stemware with the slight ruby cast to the rim that Mother saved for company. "I'm going to try walking again," he announced to our guest. "I've done the trick of getting up and down out of a chair, and I've got myself the hard-soled shoes. It's time to get going. The Berkeley Wellness Letter states flat out in no uncertain terms that inactive people are seven times more likely to suffer a stroke."

I was attempting to swallow a bite of the warm peach cake, all the time about to climb right out of my skin, with

Mother turning every other minute to gaze at me, a fixed fond smile on her face.

Sadie took the new subject in stride, dabbing her mouth with the linen napkin before she spoke. "My daddy," she told him, "had a spell of trouble with his legs, and his doctor advised him, 'Walk like you was going to school, Elam. See it in your mind's eye, that walk you used to take from the back porch of your house out there to the front door of the school. Conjure up the houses and stores you used to go past, stop the way you used to stop to wait up on somebody, and your legs will recall it. They'll be a boy's legs again and won't bother you one whit.' And that's exactly what my daddy did. It was about five, six months he did this, walked round and round in his house, which wasn't in any regard as fine and spacious a home as this, after which he never had trouble with his legs again."

"Elam," Daddy said. "There's a name."

But I thought I'd go nuts if they never let this kindly woman get to the point of her visit. "Mrs. Grimes," I said, "we are all so pleased with the proposed Agatha Adams Day at your sister's school."

Sadie looked as if she might weep with relief. "Bless you," she said. Then, speaking directly to my mother, she explained, "We are proud to be recognizing you, Mrs. Hopkins, for your fine work after all these years. We are a family of teachers, my sister and myself, and our aunts. My own mama, who was doing day work at the time Molly and I were in the county nursery program, used to credit you with setting us all on the upward path. She would quote you to us, my mama, whenever we would get down a bit at some setback, she would quote you to us as saying, 'You've got the King James Bible. You've got the language. You can do anything you want.' " She clasped her hands in her flowered lap. "The day honoring you is especially meaningful to my sister, Molly, who has just taken over as the principal of the very elementary school she was not allowed to attend when she began her education."

"I hope we can all be there for the celebration," I said.

Mother placed a hand back on my knee, giving it a squeeze. "But that's enough about those old days, don't you think, Sadie? Today I have riches enough in my lovely family. My daughter, Ella, here, always such a pretty girl, such a marvel, a young widow, raising her Robin alone in Louisiana, making a name for herself among the garden clubs as a cultivator of roses. You should have seen, Sadie, the bouquet of old roses—you know they are quite the thing now, all those bushes and climbers that used to grow alongside the road in our day or trailing up the sides of country churches—that my daughter brought me for my birthday. There were more than a dozen blooms, each the size of your fist, in the most delicate pastel shades. I have to say she's inherited my green thumb—although my own garden has been quite dried up and wilted this past year. Dear—" She turned to me, face flushed, only the slightest dampness to her eyes. "Tell Sadie about the rose you wrote me about, the special English one—"

My mouth went dry, my hands grew cold. I felt exactly like Terrell must have felt when asked to play the piano for company. Requested to display *my* ladylike talent: *rose growing.* How had my sister stood it all those years, having our mother's bright eyes fixed on her, that smile of pride and anticipation centered on her?

In a quavering voice, I performed as best I could, making a romance of the mingled cuttings of an Alba and a Damask in Hamburg, long ago when that was part of Denmark. A hardy once-flowering rose, cupped, silk-soft, blushing from deep pink to pale, transported to England. Becoming Koenigin von Danemarck, Queen of Denmark.

As the weight of my mother's expectations descended on my shoulders, there in that egg-yolk-yellow living room, with its apple-green rug and matted birds held behind non-glare glass, I wondered if my mother had invented her present life for *her* mother back in Angelina County. Writing home, *Dear Mother, Dear Mother:* letters filled with linen and flowers.

❦ Old Metairie

27

"You want a peanut butter sandwich?" Birdie asked Bailey, our new boarder.

"I hate peanut butter," he said.

"You can have banana slices or bean sprouts with it. I fix lunch on the weekend at my house."

Bailey draped himself over the straight chair at the kitchen table, enough of him left over to twist his legs into a sort of Mobius strip. "Abandoned in Purgatory, Louisiana," he moaned, "by my so-called guardian, left to fend for myself among the squatters in the middle of a national mosquito-breeding experiment."

"We don't have any jelly, though."

"I HATE PEANUT BUTTER."

"It's all right to yell now, because our tenant, Margot, she's staying with a friend of hers this weekend while Mom gets the plumber to fix her side of the house. But not when she comes back."

Bailey flung his arms across the table, hugging the far

edge. I could see that nothing in our house accommodated tall people. My nephew, naturally, had to sleep on the small blue sofa, which was not as long as he by a foot and a few inches. Plus his week here entailed other humiliations, such as sharing a bathroom with a female cousin who had lots of shampoo bottles and hairbrushes, and, because she liked to soak in the tub, a rather measly shower. My converted-from-a-closet half bath: off limits to him.

Red had come to see us off, carrying a spray of orange blossoms, which filled the car with the smell of orchards, and which he'd had to get from a florist because of the dry weather and the time of year. He still hadn't quite recovered from the piano business; surprised, as was I, by how deeply those old hurts cut. When he dropped Bailey off, he brought a wooden crate of oranges, and we peeled and ate one in full view of our children. He also left a stack of paperbacks and catalogues, and I sat up half the night reading romances: the first oranges born in the Eden of China, carried by caravan to Italy and Spain; Richard the Lion-Hearted spending the winter of 1191 in the citrus groves of Jaffa; Hawaii getting the orange from seedlings raised on shipboard by a Spanish naturalist; the Romans imagining oranges arriving in the arms of the Hesperides, who crossed the sea in a giant shell.

But now I sat studying my accounts, gnawing my lower lip. I'd abandoned any hope I'd had for jobs to appear after the mass parental return for the start of school—due to the fact that the tropical storm (still known by a female name from hurricane days) had turned us back into a swamp with tree limbs strewn around, power lines down, backyards such as mine standing ankle-deep in water, sections of the freeway closed. Flights on hold. People trying to stay afloat were not worrying themselves about the moisture level of their dozing moonflowers or about the drainage problems of their Chinese blue plumbago.

Bert, the disgruntled but becoming-wealthy plumber, was adamant this time. Which meant he was no longer taking any grief from me about my lack of discretionary funds: I had to call Roto-Rooter. Soonest. They had a waiting list, he claimed, the size of the Old Metairie phone book. Under pressure, he did admit that, yes, he had a buddy who might on a Saturday want to pick up a little extra. "Okay, sure, I'll call," he said, which he did, lining me up for late afternoon, double overtime. I didn't like letting myself into my tenant's half-house once she'd returned; it felt akin to breaking and entering. Plus she went in for a lot of aromatherapy candles so that the smell of oils and fruit and herbs and roots made for a certain faintness on my part, not all attributable to the forthcoming bills. Especially aggravating was Bert's way of saying, as he always did, "Nice place here."

With the plumber gone, I left Karl a message on his machine, thanking him for his welcome-home call and agreeing that things were too much of a mess to try to get together today. Good Karl. I wasn't ready to face seeing him—I'd had little experience with saying "sorry" to nice guys.

I found Bailey alone, Birdie having gone off to meet Felice at the Pink Mall and hang out with the older girls. Sketching something on the round table under the ceiling fan, in cargo shorts and no T-shirt, sweating front and back, his cowlick spiked in frustration. I showed him how to turn on the frosty, drippy AC unit.

"Look, Aunt Ella," he pointed, "what you need is a deck out there. See, I measured. If you put in a deck, just eight by six, with a couple of steps, you could walk, maybe you'd need a stepping-stone, from the driveway to the back door. It's a joke, wading through that pond back there."

"Look, kiddo, I'm trying to figure out how to fund the Caribbean vacation plans of the Roto-Rooter man right now. Let's do the lumber thing next time you camp out here during hurricane season."

He put down his ballpoint. Somewhere in that unhappy face a six-year-old kid sulked. "We gonna do this all the time, then?"

"What?" I decided to fix us something cold. "You can have iced coffee, ice tea, or orangeade."

"Coffee," he said, trying to sound about a hundred.

"Do what?"

"Me hanging out here so I can get to know you and the chub, like I can't see what's going on."

"I don't know. This is a first for me. Having a houseguest who'd rather be in Uzbekistan."

"Where's that?" He looked amazed and grateful to spy a slice of pound cake heading his way on a paper napkin.

"You're the scholar." We didn't keep sweets around—but that's all I knew to do for teenage boys.

"That's him who's the brain, Borden. He's the one knows it all." He looked down at the cake, and then he was wiping the last crumb from his mouth.

"He'll be in good company; everybody where he's going will know it all."

Bailey let a slight smile cross his face: his brother at Yale suddenly become just run-of-the-mill. "So what were you and Dad fighting about? Back home?"

How to answer? I felt on unsure ground. "That's hard to talk about."

He grunted and wadded up the blue paper napkin. "Nobody ever tells kids what's really going on."

No argument there. I tried not even to think about my parents in this context. "True," I admitted. I took my iced coffee and led him out back into the tropics, sitting myself down on the top step, patting the soaked board beside me. The air so muggy we could have watered plants with it. "Okay." I wanted to get this right. "Okay." I waited till he got his long limbs settled here and there on the back stoop, his knees halfway to his chest to be in my range of sight. "We were fighting, I guess you could say, about your mom."

"Mom?"

"Those of us who are younger siblings have this complex about older siblings."

He adjusted his knees. "That's news?"

"I guess I thought that your dad would never take up with the likes of me, after he'd lived with her. But what I forgot, Bailey, was that whereas we measure ourselves against them—our sister, our brother—they measure themselves against being perfect. That's a whole lot harder. I forgot the high price they pay for doing things right."

"Yeah?" He didn't look convinced.

"Anyway—" What else could I tell him?

"How'd you even meet my dad? I mean we only ever saw you and Birdie maybe a couple of times. I didn't even know, you know, that you used to know my dad."

"So many years ago, it happened in ancient times, I met your daddy. Back when he wasn't anybody's daddy. In the living room of my parents' house."

"When he was going with my mom?"

"When she first started dating him." I looked at Bailey, whose face seemed shut against the talk he'd asked for, trying to figure out how to explain. "I was just a high school kid and the only thing in the world I wanted was to get out of there, that house. Your dad helped me. He helped me run away——"

"That right?" He looked envious.

And I wondered how it would have been for these two brothers if Borden, the good older son, had stayed home, the way Terrell had, and Bailey had been the one to slip away one day, hitching a ride somewhere, forgetting to call. You never thought how it was for the one left at home when you were the one gone.

"So what about the other guy?" he asked, hooking a leg over the railing.

"Who?"

"The one, you know, you ran off with."

"Buddy."

"Him."

I sighed. None of this was simple. "Bailey, I'm forty-three years old. I've had a life. I happen to think your dad and I might make things a little better for one another."

"Yeah. Dad said."

"What did he say?"

"Sort of it wasn't my business. Sort of 'What do you know you immature, jejune punk kid? So don't have an opinion.' "

"What is your opinion?"

"Him and my mom hurt each other." He turned his back so I couldn't see his face.

"Don't we all." I said it gently, stretching my legs and studying the rotting steps.

"He must like you a lot, I guess."

"How's that?"

"Him and my mom had fights, but they never said anything about it, not to us. They pretended all the time that things were fine."

I shrugged. "Parents try to make things okay by acting like they are."

"You do that with that guy, the midget's dad?"

I took hold of my hair with both hands and lifted it, cooling my neck. "I still do that for Birdie about her daddy."

Bailey got up and messed with a yardstick, and a level he'd found which proved the back step wasn't. He shook the railing and kicked the side of the house. "Sheesh, Aunt Ella," he said, "how much could it cost? A few boards?"

"Don't ask," I told him.

28

scrambled into the house to catch the phone on the third ring. Jobs? Love? My child? The tenant? Roto-Rooter bargaining for triple overtime? Calls were never nothing in my skin-of-my-teeth life.

Hearing the rose lady's voice, I felt like a teenager being asked to the prom. My favorite client, needing me at her house right away, if I could possibly drop everything and come. She knew it was an imposition. "Ella, honestly," she pleaded needlessly, "I would not ask on such short notice if it was anything but an emergency. My husband's daddy, Teddy Senior, you know, the one with all those grain facilities, he's gone and there simply isn't time to get everyone to come in. The cats, my babies, have already been left with that exorbitant cat sitter till I could just—"

"This afternoon?" I breathed out in relief.

"Could you, Ella, do you think? I'm programming your code into the back door at this very minute. And there are those pesky water bottles. If you could come, I mean now? And we could go over everything? In the time it takes me to write it all down? Be a dear—?"

I was a dear. Dashing toward the bedroom to pretty up a

bit, change into good shorts, mess with my oak-brown snarls, screw my head on.

"Where are you going?" Bailey, who'd trailed inside after me, watched as I grabbed my car keys.

"Job," I told him. "Manna. Funds. We can run the AC night and day."

"Give me a sec, will you, to get my shoes on?"

I wheeled around in my doorway. Having forgotten that strays were not privy to the ground rules of the house. "You stay," I said. I'd not even ever taken Birdie, nor would I ever take anyone along on a job. I could never take that risk, bringing someone who could break, drop, slosh, move, any precious fixed or growing thing. Or, as youth did, want to talk at my most concentrated moment.

"What do you mean, stay? Here? By myself?" My nephew sounded close to panic.

"Not only that, and keep the back door closed meantime, you need to listen for the Roto-Rooter truck, and let him in the front half of the duplex. See, the key's on this chain, hanging right here." I stepped back and waved a hand at the key rack by the back door.

"But what'll I do? What if somebody—?"

"Bailey, have you ever been alone two milliseconds in your whole life?" I threw up my hands. "I don't know what you'll 'do.' Place a lot of phone calls and charge them to your dad's phone. Redesign my back porch. Wait for Birdie and her friend Felice."

I pulled into the Georgian colonial's driveway like a horse dashing to the stable. Home again. Mrs. Thibaud threw open the back door and gave me a little hug, this client not much older than I was, who'd already lugged the six cobalt-blue water bottles into the kitchen by herself. The whole water-purification industry gone into overtime with this last tropical storm, sending over machines and person-power to help with the reverse-osmosis units and to check the filtration and purification systems. Water, its control and management, a more lucrative business on our part of the coast than cotton. And no way, it seemed, to pipeline our excess straight to Texas's parched acres.

She held up a list she'd been writing on, apparently standing at the kitchen phone center. Lovely blue-tiled floors, lovely all-stainless ovens and sinks. Everywhere, small vases of "my" low-country roses.

Being back came as such a thrill, a relief, that it took a full minute at least for what I was seeing with my own eyes to register. Mrs. Thibaud had on her slim body the very black, button-front linen dress I'd once stolen. I couldn't breathe. Everything grew dim. I thought perhaps I'd pass out on the spot. The whole thing had been a ruse. She'd brought me back here to accuse; next, the thrift shop green linen I'd tucked away upstairs would be brought out and waved in my face. I thought of getting right down on my knees and telling all.

"I hate funerals." She appeared to still be talking. "I wore this to my own daddy's funeral and I'm going to burn it, I absolutely am, after Teddy Senior's service. Make a bonfire. They wear white in some countries, don't they? I know they do. India? But then"—she had to stop and wipe her eyes—"they burn the body with the dress."

"Oh," I murmured. "Oh, Mrs. Thibaud. I wonder, if I

could, if I could presume, if you'd let me buy that dress from you, after your, your tragic event? It's the very one I especially need to go to a ceremony honoring my mother in East Texas at the end of next month. You know how you can't wear light colors after Labor Day? And I don't really have anything appropriate, I mean the black things I do—" I was babbling. "Please, I'm sure I'm out of line, I'm sure. I just thought—" I wanted to trade clothes with her at that very moment. She'd fit right into my best cuffed tan shorts and white camp shirt, and show them off better than I did.

"Ella, Lord, yes. Take the thing. You're welcome to it. It has nothing but sad memories for me. Look, I'll leave it here, on this shelf, after we get back from the cemetery. We're going to go away for a few days and recuperate, this has been the worst, sorriest summer in my whole—Did you see our garage-door opener is on the blink from all the power outages?" She stared at me, a stricken look on her face. "There, Ella, what's wrong with me? You said your mother. Did you lose your mother and I'm running on like this? What possesses me?"

I felt light-headed. I had that button-front black dress in my sights. "No, no," I assured her. "I didn't mean to say, what I meant, a ceremony, it's just a sort of—of reunion for these ladies, a fifty-year reunion for a group of girls who used to call themselves the Hanky Club. Pen pals. They'd send each other—"

But she'd moved on—my mother apparently still breathing and so not in need of our prayers—to explaining about how to feed the rare Chartreux cats without frightening them. "Did I tell you about this extortionist I hired? To look after my babies? At a fee I won't even suggest. That woman would *pull them out from under the bed*! For what I paid her! You just tear open the packets and leave them here, see, these blue saucers. No need to go upstairs, you understand? Now here's where we are, in St. John the Baptist Parish, a number, but no need to call unless this place is up in flames. And my roses—"A dreamy smile came over her golf-tanned face. "Well, they always seem to droop a bit after you've been here and gone. I don't know if I water them too much or not enough. I don't have that touch. I read somewhere people talked to flowers? Do you do that?" She smiled, a very blond, made-up woman with a lot of energy and general good feeling, who might, in another life, have made a first-class waiter at the Pink Cafe.

Left alone, I took off my sandals so my feet could enjoy the cool marble floor on the way to the rose-filled atrium. There I simply stood for the longest time, letting the chlorine settle out of the water in the long-necked sprinkle cans. Walking around to see where the natural light came through the skylights as we headed toward the autumnal equinox, as we headed, surely, toward drier weather and a sunny Indian summer. How glad I was to see again the little pink sweetheart Cécile Brünner, the blushing old Noisette, Aimee Vibert, the porcelain and ivory English hybrids. Breathing deep the mingled scents of steeped tea, myrrh, bananas, spice, musk: the many perfumes of the fragrant, ever-blooming country roses.

Upstairs, I headed straight for the closet, scene of my past crimes. There, in the row of black linen dresses, a space, much as I had left before Terrell's service when I'd borrowed the crisp and proper garment. Further back, the shoulder-streaked celadon linen, still acting as undergarment, garment-in-waiting, for the splashy, frogged, emerald brocade.

Joy in my heart, at the thought of full reparation concerning the purloined dress soon to be properly in my possession, I greeted the pair of cats I'd spoken with on two occasions before. "No need," I said, as they lay on their sides, lithe and langorous yellow-eyed felines, "for me to come up here anymore. And my apologies for disturbing your naps on my earlier visits. I'll be preparing a small repast for you downstairs, some gourmet—it appears from the nature of the foil container—version of the common cat's Tender Vittles. Take care."

In the kitchen, I left each a rose petal in her blue bowl of water, and, on the blue dinner saucers, mixed half an egg yolk each into the moist preformed food, the telltale shell whisked away in the disposal.

Patting the shelf where soon my dress would appear, I bent and kissed each cobalt-blue bottle of fresh designer water.

29

I cut my hair. A gesture right up there with Birdie shaving her legs, and perhaps out of the same impulse: to look *nice*. Now that it didn't matter anymore. Now that my tangles no longer gave me distance. How could I never have guessed that being approved of by my mother would leave me so much more defenseless, exposed, than being disapproved of? How could I not have seen what freedom I had as the black sheep, the prodigal daughter? No wonder my sister had wanted a secret life that no one could touch. And me, all those years, never offering her sympathy, never offering her thanks.

I had on my white camp shirt, which I'd worn to my unexpected watering job, and Birdie and Felice had donned theirs, used for String Project performances, though they'd kept on baggy shorts. I'd had to call Karl to cadge a white dress shirt for Bailey—who else did I know his size?—since he had certainly not brought such a garment on his slumming trip to the bayou.

"Ecccchhh," the boy had said, when I handed it to him, sniffing the shirt the way a dog sniffs another dog. "Couldn't I just buy one or something at the dinky pinky mall? I don't need to wear a shirt some dude has *worn*."

"Tell him not to sweat all over it, will you?" Karl had asked, poking it grudgingly out his car window, promising to call me later.

Mayfair was taking us to the Old Metairie Country Club, dressing us all alike, using us as helpers to deliver the all-pink pre-deb ball gowns. Her way of doing something special for Birdie's visiting cousin, and of acknowledging his daddy's wonderful gift.

She and I had already talked about Red's offer of the new cello and flute, the night I got back from Texas, after Birdie had been on the phone half an hour pouring out the good news to Felice. "I cannot let you do that," Mayfair had objected. "I cannot let you buy my girl an instrument costing two thousand dollars."

"Listen," I'd reminded her, "I couldn't buy my own daughter a two-*hundred*-dollar cello. I'm standing here with the AC on, hearing the dollars go by, planning to finance a time-share in the Caymans for my plumber. But this is not from me; this is from the daddy of the boy I'll be sitting, Birdie's Uncle Rufus, my sister's husband. He's doing this for his own private reasons."

"You mean guilt?"

"Something like that." I explained that the deal was strictly with Birdie, she'd done the negotiating, how much he was putting in, what the girls had saved, what was still lacking.

"I can manage the difference. Let me at least do that."

"You are not to put in a cent and I'm not either."

"I'll have to come up with a treat, then. Take you along to one of my parties or something."

This afternoon, late, she met us in front of the club with a large van and two other helpers, also in white shirts, her costumers. She had a permit for me to place on the dashboard of my less than elegant car. We clustered together, our feet damp but back in their shoes. Our girls were not overly impressed with the spectacular pink Moorish edifice at the end of the long, divided, oak-canopied street. The String Project had never played there; it couldn't be anyplace they needed to go.

I gave Mayfair a proper introduction to Bailey, who, a gentleman despite himself, shook her hand and thanked her for inviting us.

"My, you are one good-looking boy," she said. "These girls inside will flip at the sight of you. You Texas boys." She threw up her hands. "Once upon a time, a zillion years ago, I married one myself."

Our job, now, was to get the varying-shades-of-pink ball gowns delivered safely, one-of-a-kind designs in irreplaceable fabrics, all securely sealed in plastic bags. "Don't track," Mayfair directed. "Wipe your feet inside the door." Her reddish hair freshly plaited, in a russet smock, she was very much in charge, checking with the club manager and the young, brisk pink-party planner.

Following after her, we looked like the bearers of a feast in ancient days, all with our arms outstretched, holding treasures out in front of us, high off the ground, our offerings. Approaching the castlelike interior, we went under a very long pink awning, wide enough to shelter three couples abreast, flanked by large pots of pink geraniums fresh from the florist. Inside, we went past, but not into, the men-only grill, through the Petit Wedgwood Room, across a dark lounge with the imported thirty-six-foot pewter bar and inlaid pewter wall panels for which the club was noted. In the back sunroom, the dozen girls waited, barefoot, in short shorts, their hair on giant rollers. Taking no more notice of Bailey than they did of the rest of us—we were functionaries—they found their names on the plastic bags and headed off to the dressing rooms. Mayfair Roberdeau following along to be sure things were all in order.

I wandered around with Bailey and the girls, nobody seeming to mind or even notice we were there. Upstairs on the wraparound porch, the pots of ginger, whose scent I had imagined, were gone. In their place, massed pink geraniums and impatiens. And, along with the pots and their fragrance of spice, gone was any wish on my part to make an anecdote of this outing for my mother. What did it matter now, impressing her?

We looked down onto six green-clay courts, partially covered in tarps. Bailey, a tennis player, pointed out small footbaths for washing the soles of athletic shoes. "The courts are made from Tennessee clay," he said. "You track green." Taking in the seats for spectators and the grand reviewing stand, he muttered, "Fucking Wimbledon." Below us, a couple of water-system trucks were working away with hoses snaking into the building while another truck guided hoses sucking up the floodwater on the patio. We could see the golf course, with a few men playing through despite what must be damage to the greens, and, toward the bayou, the sloping lawn I fancied they used for Easter-egg hunts, slippery with mud.

Heading for the entrance, Bailey hung back, letting the girls race ahead to find Mayfair. "You come here?" he asked me.

"Surely you jest."

"This isn't that far from your house. It's like—close."

"Far?"

"You know what I mean." He shifted around from one foot to the other, his tanned face straining with the effort to speak my language.

"You mean, how come this isn't in another part of town from where I live?"

"Sort of."

How to put these niceties to an Austin boy, used to the clearer demarcations of West Lake Hills and Pflugerville? "Probably," I searched for words, "some people in the antebellum homes on that wide shady street out there *can't* come here, and probably some people a couple of blocks from me in those little pastel places with the magnolia trees *can*. It's not, ummm, in the Deep South, it's not money, or just money. Or mainly money."

"That right?"

"I don't know, Bailey. How do I know? I'm just passing on an impression. Buddy, Birdie's daddy, made his living repossessing yachts. He dealt with a lot of new money, some old. What he said to me was, you couldn't tell. You couldn't figure it out if you were outside it, and if you were inside it, you didn't need to."

The tall boy, used to privilege, looked around the vast club, now filled with pink-clothed tables and topiary trees whose branches held pink carnations and velvet bows. "I guess they have stuff like members-only Sunday brunches, and members-only monthly suppers. Stuff like that?"

"You seem to know these matters." I wondered if he was thinking of the sailing club.

He stopped and rolled up the sleeves of his borrowed shirt. "What happens if, you know, somebody gets a divorce?"

Apparently he was. I stopped at the front doors. "Mayfair says the memberships are in the men's names."

"Yeah." He nodded. "I thought."

"You're thinking of your mom?"

"She really got mad when Dad moved out." He looked everywhere but at me.

Outside, the girls appeared to be trying equally hard to communicate with Mayfair.

"Ms. Roberdeau," Birdie was saying, "we bet that was your aunt who came to visit my grandmom in Austin."

"You said she went to see her teacher, Mama——" Felice chimed in.

"Hang on here." Mayfair shook her head. "Slow down. The lady my auntie went to see, in Shreveport it was, had already been taken to the funeral home by the time she got there."

"But you said that your mama and her couldn't go to the school they wanted to, Mama. You said——" Felice tugged on her mother's shirt.

"And Mrs. Grimes, who came to see my grandmom, she and her sister, they couldn't go to the school they wanted to." Birdie rocked up and down on her feet, looking at me for confirmation.

Ella in Bloom

"Oh, children," Mayfair said, her voice gentle, the pink Moorish country club immense in the muggy air behind her, "back in those days there were lots and lots of little girls who couldn't go to the schoolhouse of their choice."

Unbidden, tears filled my eyes. How little any of us understood the generations that came before. I thought of Bailey, trying to figure out his mom and dad, and of our girls here, straining to connect their segregated pasts. I thought of myself, Ella, and the parents I would never know.

30

Hello, Bird," Karl said, letting himself in the back door. "Who's this?"

"This is my cousin, Bailey. Bailey, this is Karl."

"He giving you any trouble?"

Birdie shook her head. "I imagine you don't have cousins."

"The head cheerleader at my high school had a cousin; he had a glass eye."

Birdie giggled, and my nephew rose to stare down the unexpected male intruder. Then, remembering his manners, he stuck out a hand, mumbling, "Thanksfortheshirt," without a lot of conviction, shoving it in the visitor's direction, like a ball of rags.

"Your old man's Uncle Rufus, have I got that right?"

"Yeah," Bailey allowed.

Karl sniffed the shirt and tucked it under his arm. "Around here, I'm Uncle Karl."

"Okay," Bailey said. "You want to sit or something?"

"Count me out. I got a house to show your aunt, is that right, your aunt?" He looked at me. "It's not great, but it's got a story."

"Sure," I said, glad he'd waited to show up until Birdie got home from school. Bailey, it had turned out, did best with a keeper. "I've been watering. Let me clean up——?"

"I'll swing by a place I need to look at on Jasmine Lane."

"No need to swim back to the door." I gestured to the loafers in his hand. "I'll meet you in the driveway."

While I fixed up a bit, plus wondered how it would be, leaving these two alone, if my daughter would do her house guest any major damage, I heard the pair having a go at playing sibling.

"My mom sometimes goes to the movies with Karl," Birdie told him.

"Your mom sometimes goes to the movies with any creep who asks."

I heard a smack, and looked in to see Bailey falling to his knees as if shot, clutching his Adam's apple. "The attack of the little people." He rolled onto his back. "Say good-bye, Earth, I'm gone."

"Take it back." Birdie put her foot on his chest.

"I take it back. Your mom only goes when the creep asks her nice."

I left the cousins caterwauling, a word of my daddy's which I assumed meant *cat fight*. Daddy's language had been floating around in my mind ever since I got home, trying to shake off the Texas trip.

In my black T-shirt and blue-and-black skirt, my straw bag on my head like someone fording the Nile, sandals in my hand, umbrella under my arm, I waited in the driveway for Karl.

As soon as I opened the door of the Honda and climbed into the passenger seat, I could tell something was up. No chewing gum either in progress or on the dash. No pencil between his white realtor's teeth. And the unmistakable (and awful) smell in his spotless show-car of air freshener. Karl was smoking again.

"Lung cancer," I said, fastening the double seat belt.

"I'm fine, thanks," he said.

"If you have any Juicy Fruit left over, I'll take a stick." That was self-defense.

He motioned to the map compartment, where I found three packs of cigarettes and two packs of gum. I unpeeled a stick. "Where are we going?"

"Middle America." He backed out and whipped over to the through street, taking us out of our safe, secure (soggy) neighborhood, through a couple of equally wet, adjacent neighborhoods whose children went to lesser schools and were taught by teachers who probably also favored aroma-therapy candles and whose plumbing probably had also needed the services of an overtime professional.

"Friendly kid back there, who smelled up my shirt. Glad he's not Bird's beau. Got the personality of a first try: tongue-tied and chilled-out."

"He's having a hard time."

"He look like his dad?"

"Karl," I said. Sooner or later we'd have to get to the matter, but I didn't want him baiting me. "So what's the house you wanted me to see?"

"Only one I'm buying, that's all." He sounded smug.

"You're kidding. What brought this on?"

"One guess." He dodged a pothole. "Opportunity."

"That's great."

The house, in an area north and west of Old Metairie, at this moment blockaded off with sawhorses because the streets were flooded, had a SOLD sign in the yard. We parked on a shoulder, the only dry ground, and, shoes back in hand, walked the block to the one-and-a-half-story frame house. Which had a battered cottonwood in the yard, a dangling shutter from last night's big blow, and an enclosed garage in the back that had been turned, it looked like, into a guest house or rental.

Inside, the place smelled damp; okay, it smelled faintly of mildew. And something else. Bats? Mold?

"Your depressed daddy left you his life's savings?" I asked, indicating my awe at the size and condition of the fairly new builder's house.

Karl looked at me, glum. "My dad wouldn't get up out of that easy chair if there was a million dollars for the taking on the dining room table. My mom says he wouldn't put his foot out if it was on fire. I try to tell her: it's clinical."

After the tour of the three/two-and-a-half with all-built-in kitchen and a wet bar in the living room, plus washer-dryer connections upstairs and down, plus a gas-burning fake fireplace, we sat on the front steps, with only a slight drip from the roof above hitting our heads.

Karl looked at me, then up at the gray sky, spit on his finger and held it up to tell which way the wind was blowing as his hand bent horizontal in a sudden gust from the Gulf Coast squall. He fished out a cigarette, turned his back to the gale, lit up, and took a deep, audible drag. He jiggled his octopus of realtor's keys. "You want to hear about the house?"

"Every detail."

"Why it didn't sell? Otherwise I couldn't buy so much as that ripped-off shutter there, right? I don't know if you saw, driving over, there's a Lutheran church on the corner and there's a Unitarian church on the next block, and then there's another different variety of Lutheran half a block past that. Nobody wants to live with all those churches. It gives them the willies. That's what I hear. But every owner here's been a one-family/two-kids: teacher, barber, pharmacist, high school yearbook photographer. If you take out inflation, the price of the house has not varied in relation to the market one thin dime in the forty years since it was built. This area is not going up and it's not going down. It's not going anywhere."

"It's a sure thing. No gamble." I tried to smile.

"You got it." He looked pleased, and pulled on his smoke. "What'd you think? Think there's enough room for three? A private bath for Birdie?"

I couldn't believe he meant it. "You can't mean that," I said. "You know we're not, we were never—"

"I thought maybe, if we had a place big enough—"

"Karl," I said, "I slept with Uncle Rufus."

"You what? Come on."

"You must have known. Since he came here to visit, we've—"

"If you recall, please," he said, "we're talking not all that long ago. Just the minute he left your place, you picked up the phone and invited me over for some serious stuff."

He was right. I had. I'd called him, hurt and angry because Red had had his mind on Mr. Emu all through our fine dinner at the Pink Cafe. "I'm sorry," I said.

"Bird know this?"

"I believe so."

"That tongue-tied beanpole know it?"

"I suspect."

"Then how come I'm just now hearing about it? The guy who just bought a house for who he thought was his future family? Tell me that? Tell me how come?" He was yelling.

"Things changed in Texas."

"He got a lot of money, is that it?"

"If I'd been after money, would I have been pimping plumbers for my tenant?"

"What's he got, then? What's he got I haven't got?" He threw his cigarette into the squishy yard and lit another. "A kid. *He's got a kid.*" He looked stabbed.

I let out my breath, knotting my hands. "Two. Two boys."

He rose to his feet and bellowed out at the strong Gulf wind. "*He's got two kids.* Now you've got three. And I don't have one. Not one single kid, and me staring at fifty."

I pulled him back down to the wet step. Remembering how devastated I'd been when Buddy inherited a trio and I didn't have any and wasn't likely to get any. And now here I was, doing the same thing to my friend Karl. I knew how bad that hurt, to think your time has come and gone. And it was too late, for both of us, for me to give him one the way Buddy had for me. "I'm sorry," I said again, not knowing how to let him know I understood.

He began to tear up his cigarettes one by one, dropping them in a neat pile. "You know what my mom said to me? She said, 'If you don't have a kid, you'll turn out just like your pa.' I told her, 'He *had* a kid, and he turned out like he did. Maybe he'd of been a golf pro if he hadn't.' That just came to me, *golf pro.* That had a good ring."

"Uncle Rufus and I go way back," I said. "It's like not losing all those years."

"All those years?" He wiped his eyes, getting tobacco shreds on his cheeks. "What about all these years I lost? What about that?"

"You didn't lose them. We helped each other out. You showed me your houses. I got a little support with Birdie. That's not losing. Birdie likes you."

He bawled. "That's the way of it. You get attached. You can't help it. I saw this house, I know it's got an iffy location and cheesy construction, and I thought, hell, that's my job, finding people the houses that are going to fix their lives. Why not mine for a change? I said. Why not fix mine for a change? You think I don't know I been treading water ever since my divorce? You think I don't know living in my folks' garage apartment is a death wish? You think I don't know you didn't have intention one of ever moving in with me and ironing my shirts and making me carry out the garbage? You think I didn't know somebody with kids was gonna show up on your falling-down doorstep one day?"

"I liked you, too," I said.

"You did? Sure you did. I was okay, wasn't I?"

"You were definitely okay."

He rubbed around on his face, shifted the shoulders of his realtor's jacket. He fished out a packet of gum and handed me a stick. Peace offering. "I should of married the head cheerleader," he said. "She'd of had half a dozen."

31

Bailey had just spent at least ten minutes on the phone with Karl. Right, Karl. Hanging up in frustration, he said, "Gross. He asked me to go to the movies with him. What's he think, just because I wore his slimy shirt, we're going to hook up? Gross." He reached his arms across the kitchen table, hugging the other side, banging his chin on the wood.

"Karl likes movies," I explained. I'd come back from seeing him earlier in the week, shut the door of my room, dodging still-spatting cousins, and cried into my pillow, for all those things in our lives that never worked out. For "Uncle Karl," the gum-chewing realtor, who had been assured that he'd be welcome at our house anytime.

"Forget it," Bailey muttered. "I'll buy him another shirt. He said I ruined it. Sheesh, it wasn't even *cotton*."

Piecing it together, from what I could hear of his end and what he related, he'd called Karl to ask him, Why couldn't they get a few boards and put up a six-foot-by-eight-foot deck for his Aunt Ella while he was here, you know, be a help. To which Karl had spelled out all the reasons why not: wood rotted, then you had rotten wood with water collecting underneath, bugs gone to heaven, starting to smell, don't even consider it. Come back and see us at Mardi Gras, kid, beautiful down here then. Ask your aunt. When pressed, Karl had then explained that you had to bring in a load of topsoil, make some runoff channels, cover it with gravel, and then fit your bricks on top of that: drainage. He could show Bailey, he had a couple of houses he could let him see how they handled the backyard problem. He could also let him look at a half a dozen designer homes nobody was showing during flood season. Forget it, Bailey told him. Then Karl had asked: "You interested in that lizard flick?"

The idea of being driven around, however, was not as insulting to my nephew-in-residence as it might have been earlier in the week. I'd let my boarder borrow my car late on Wednesday afternoon. He had decided to take his cousin to the Pink Mall for a double Blue Bell Supreme ice cream cone, since he was going stir-crazy. I'd given him the keys and a map, and offered to mark the route to the small mall.

"Give me a break," he'd said, trying to burn rubber (not an easy task on a driveway standing in water) backing out. Needless to say, they'd got totally lost and arrived home (coneless in Purgatory) one hour later. Birdie, who knew the way on foot, didn't know how to help him out, since she took a lot of shortcuts cars couldn't make. As the mockingbird flew and Birdie walked, it wasn't over half a mile. But Bailey hadn't reckoned with the Byzantine dogleg streets designed to keep transients, strangers, all outsiders out. Again and again he'd encounted such paper-clip double loops as Magnolia Drive turning into Magnolia Lane and then Magnolia Circle and Magnolia Place. A coil of streets you had to retrace if you once got confused and took the wrong turn.

Today I'd promised him, after Birdie got back from the first fall String Project practice, a trip to a beautiful show-place. It was Saturday, and Red was due to come retrieve his younger son tonight or tomorrow, depending on what kind of time he made. And all of us were eager to see him.

"Look at that sun," I told Bailey, gesturing to a faint increase in light visible out the kitchen door. "We'll go to Belle Vue and you can meet my friend Henry."

"Not another one." He folded his arms over his head.

"Not another one. This is a gardener who taught me all I know about roses."

"Beats me having a date with Karl," he groused, kicking the table leg.

I felt happy to be again at *the source,* and paid our nominal fees, leading the children leisurely past the long reflecting pool, the lily-pad pond with its hundred varieties of fern, the English country garden, the hummingbird garden, to the bower of climbing roses, dozens of kinds, at the end of which there was Henry. Just as I'd last seen him. Wearing knee pads, pail and implements by his side, gloves tucked in the back pocket of his work pants, hands muddy.

I introduced him to the cousins. "This is my daughter, Birdie," I said, "and this is my nephew Bailey Hall. You met his daddy, Rufus." And to them I explained, "This is my friend Henri Legrand. The head rose gardener at Belle Vue, and the great-great-grandson of the Empress Josephine's gardener."

Was that true? Did it matter? It could have been true.

Sometimes, I concluded, it was all right to say what could have been true.

"Hello, Mr. Legrand," Birdie said. "My mom talks about you."

"My dad came here——?" Bailey asked.

"Good to see you, Ella, and to meet your young ones." Henry stood, his knees creaking a bit, and shook hands with both of my charges. Then, getting back down again with effort, he said, "Here, boy, hold this for me. Take care, there's thorns."

Bailey reached out, a little taken aback, and, sure enough, got stuck and yelped. "Sorry, sir," he said, taking a handkerchief out of his back pocket and holding the large bush over the hole.

"Use my gloves if you have the need," Henry said. "My own fingers quit feeling that prick a long time ago. These beauties nearly drowned this week. I can't dig them all up. That's too costly and too risky. But this is one of my prizes, and it's a compact plant. I'm taking the chance." The coppery yellow color of the Mlle. Franziska Krüger seemed to tremble in the thin sunlight, as if expecting more rain. He put down what looked like crumpled net in the bottom of the hole, and then had Bailey set the shrub back in place.

"That okay?" Bailey asked, the handkerchief showing red.

"Push it down a bit, son. A bit more. Act like you're plugging it in the ground. There you go."

Bailey held it with one hand, and helped to make a moat of soil around it with the other. He wiped his forehead, streaking it with dirt.

"Appreciate that," Henry said, moving over crab fashion to a velvety red Tea, the Frances Dubriel, draining the water and shaping a new trough. "What about you, boy?" he asked. "What do you do with yourself?"

Before Bailey could answer, while he stood there hurting from the puncture wound to his palm, Birdie said, "He's dropping out for a while, my cousin is, Mr. Legrand."

"That right?" Henry asked, keeping his eyes on what his hands were about.

Bailey looked as if he could fall right through the ground. He shot my daughter a glance that would have made birds plunge from the sky.

"He's investigating his options," she explained.

"That right?" With effort, Henry dug around and righted a rosebush I didn't recognize, a creamy white. He told me it was a Bourbon that had China blood in it, mixed with a Damask. And I realized it was one I'd written about to my mother.

With effort, he got back to his feet, bending over to rub one knee. "I met this boy's dad, as I recall. That right, Ella?"

"Yes," I said.

"What does he think about a big strong boy like you crapping out?" He took his straw hat off and smacked his leg with it.

Bailey stepped back as if hit. "I guess, you know, my brother's at Yale. I guess Dad doesn't, doesn't——" He looked as if he couldn't find a well-mannered way to say "give a fuck," or "give a shit." "I guess he's pretty busy," he said. "My mom, my mom died in January."

"Sorry, son," Henry said, reaching out and taking the

hand wrapped in the handkerchief. "I was talking to myself, more than likely, thinking about my own self back there in the dark ages. Here—" He opened Bailey's palm and pushed on the wound. "Suck on it," he said. "Thorns are bad as snakebites. You got to treat them the same way."

I gave Henry a thank-you hug, promised to come back soon, and we left him, indeed looking like a farmer in the Rhône Valley, bent over his prize old roses.

When we were back through the trellises, Bailey stopped. "I embarrassed you, didn't I, Aunt Ella?"

"No, you didn't."

"Henry thought I was a rich prick, didn't he?"

"He was coming from his experience—"

"Everybody thinks that. I'm not good for squat. The gnome here with the flapping mouth, she's got a big talent she can tell everybody about. And my bro can say, 'I got in Yale.' He doesn't have to be planning to do jack shit with his life, all he has to say is, 'I got in Yale.' 'Hi, I'm at Yale.' 'Hi, I play the doo-wah-doo cello.' "

"That's how I felt about your mom," I told him.

He looked off past the reflecting pool. "Even when she quit playing?"

"You never get over being the younger kid," I said.

Birdie stood in front of him. "That's at your old place in West Lake Hills you were Borden's brother, Bailey, which you were always complaining about having to be. But in your new place, in Pflugerville, nobody knows who you are. So you can be whoever you want to be."

My nephew put his hand on her head and lightly hammered it with his other hand, as if driving a post into the ground. "Do not tell me one more piece of helpful crap about my life, Troll. Do not open your mouth in my direction one single more time."

Birdie giggled and took the door key she wore on a ribbon around her neck and poked it in her ear, pretending to turn herself off.

Bailey laughed in spite of himself. "Lucky, I guess, you just had one, *Ella.*"

And hearing him use just my name, like that, which seemed a sort of permission to take up with his dad, I broke my never-touch-teenagers rule and, at the gate, reached up and slicked down his cowlick.

32

The kids and I had early spaghetti and saved Red some. Hoping against hope that the phone wouldn't ring with the news that he'd stopped somewhere to the east of us for the night.

Birdie, the first to the back door when he knocked, threw herself at him, giving him, on tiptoe, a big choke around the neck. "Hi, Un—Hi, *Rufus.*" She blushed furiously at the intimacy of his bare name.

"Hi, yourself," he said, setting down his shoes, his feet wet, suitcase in hand.

"You're supposed to say 'Guten Tag,' that's what Granddaddy does."

"How about 'Buenas noches'?"

"Okay."

"Hello, Red." I kissed him right there. Youth could look the other way if they wanted to.

"Hello, Ella." He looked happy to see me. "It's good to be home."

While I filled his plate and opened him a beer, Birdie pulled him into a kitchen chair, barely giving him time to sit before she began to talk. "*Today we found our instruments.* Felice's mom took us to the city to the violin shop and the orchestra shop. This old man showed me everything about good cellos. I got to touch the wrapped metal strings and the gut strings—they call them catgut but they're really sheep intestines—and sit and hold it between my knees, the way they did in the old days, and the way Yo-Yo Ma does when he is playing an old instrument. And I got to try a twenty-thousand-dollar cello and even pull the foot down so it fit me."

She scooted her chair till it touched his, transfixed with excitement. "I told him I had two thousand, and first he showed me one with an Italian name that was plywood with this veneer that made it look real antique. I said I wouldn't buy something made out of plywood no matter how it looked, that I wanted the same thing you always got in good instruments of the violin family, and that's spruce wood on the front and maple on the back and sides and neck. And he acted like he didn't have one for me. They had one for three thousand, he said, that was German with a pretend Italian name. But I said that was too much. Then his old wife, she was shorter than me, came up to him and said"—Birdie got out of her chair and crouched down, craning up her neck as if talking to someone very tall, speaking in a heavy accent— " 'Zhow er zee one on conzignment.' And he got out this other new cello that was Korean, and it had an Italian name, too, the way they all do, and it was a Strad copy the way they all are, but the back and sides and neck were maple, and the neck scroll was very beautiful, and the front was spruce. He said it was eighteen hundred dollars, and I told him I would like to have that one."

Red looked pleased.

"And Felice, at the orchestra store, they offered her a copy of a four-piece Bressan flute made out of grenadilla wood, but it was a copy of a Baroque flute, and she wanted a modern one. Then the man showed her a Japanese open-hole flute with all-silver body and stops, that had the same construction as one for eight thousand, for two thousand. And Felice said, 'I'll take that.' Because she was forgetting that we didn't exactly have two thousand, and because she was a lot in love with it."

She stood close to Red and put her hand on his shoulder. "So, Un—So, Rufus, that means we are missing two hundred dollars from having enough for two instruments. And Felice's mom wanted to pay, but we said, No, that wasn't right. So you have to let Bailey come back for five days, and then that'll be the rest of what we need."

"Trapped in Purgatory with the pubes," Bailey groaned, throwing his arms around his own bony shoulders, but he didn't really seem to mind.

When Red agreed to all the details of the terms, and wrote Birdie a check for what they'd bargained, she looked as if she might die of rapture, and nearly strangled him saying thanks.

After she'd gone off, dragging the miles of twisted phone cord behind her, to tell Felice the news, Bailey opened himself a beer (without asking me) and sat down across from his dad. "How'd it go with nano-brain?" he asked, in a super casual voice.

"He said, 'Tell my bro to write when he learns how.' "

Red gave his younger son a sort of shoulder punch of affection, in the oblique male manner. "I hated leaving him there, to tell the truth."

"How come?" Bailey affected disinterest.

Red considered. He looked tired from the long trip, but more relaxed than he had in Texas. "I'm a country boy, I guess. They looked—tough—to me, the other freshmen I saw. I don't mean like rough, just that prep-school, team-player demeanor, both the girls and the boys. The kind of look I take as: Who are you, hick? But that's projecting. Your brother—"

"Sure. He's a jock. He's cool."

"What've you been up to?" Red asked.

"Uh, I had it in my head," Bailey began to explain, "to build Ella a deck. To do something here, you know, to help out. In Texas, you put up a redwood deck or a cedar deck or any kind of deck, you end up with a *deck*. Here, you've got a pond in your yard with rotten wood floating in it. Eccchhh." He tilted his chair back, taking a long pull on his beer. "So this afternoon, we went to this old mansion, I guess you'd call it? That's been there for a hundred and fifty years and now you pay to see it? The first thing I noticed was: *no standing water.* Zip. I had to check how they did that. First of all, they've got this reflecting pool, and framing it all around, two foot wide, they've got gravel, boxed in and sloping a little so all the water runs down to this hedge. And under the hedge where you don't notice, they have drains. Me and Ella talked to this guy, this gardener, Mr. Legrand—"

"I met Henry," Red said, reaching out a hand and finding mine. "He made quite an impression."

"That's right, he said." Bailey stopped a minute, blinked, reminded of the painful scene at Belle Vue. "Yeah, anyhow, he was keeping these roses from washing away by building them up into, like, anthills, and then making a trough around them with a canal on one side that let the water run off. And at the sides of every rose bed, he'd got long ditches, like irrigation ditches, that emptied into drains. The thing is, in Texas, you catch every drop of water you can; here, you got to have runoff."

"I see that," Red said, sticking out his leg with its damp pants cuff.

"So, uhh," Bailey continued, looking somewhere over his dad's shoulder, draining almost half of his bottle of beer, "I thought when I came back here over Christmas break, I could, you know, fix Ella up something so we don't have to fucking wade everywhere."

What a roundabout way boys had of telling adults about major life matters. Here, woven into his talk of coastal saturation, the sixteen-year-old beanpole with the stand-up hair and the attitude had just announced the happy news that he wouldn't be dropping out of school after all. Plus that he had plans to come see his young cousin and her mom in this scruffy, moated half-a-house again.

To which wonderful revelations, Red responded in the unflapped way of the daddies of sons, "You'll have to bring in some topsoil, I imagine."

"Yeah, I figured. Build it up."

Red rolled up the sleeves of his white shirt, his left arm a dark tan from driving with the window down. I spotted it because my daddy used to do the same, to and from the university. Rolling down the sleeves of his blue shirts, knotting and cinching his yellow ties when it was time for the classroom. "Where are the oranges?" Red asked, looking around.

The words brought a blush to my cheeks, as if this were our code for lovemaking, though I knew he meant the crate of assorted kinds he'd sent. "I ate them," I said. "We did, ate them all."

He smiled at me. "They're growing more all over the world," he told me.

Then at that moment, I heard the *blat-blat* horn of a familiar Honda. But what could Karl be thinking? To come pull in behind Red's car and honk? I rose, half angry, half embarrassed, getting ready to charge out the back door. But Bailey jumped to his feet and, grabbing his tennis shoes, said, "Gee, Dad, we thought you weren't coming back till tomorrow, and, uh, Birdie and I already had plans to see *Godzilla* with Karl."

He stuck his head in Birdie's room and made wild gestures for her to come on, hurry up.

Red looked at his son, disbelieving. "That the guy who used to take Ella out?"

"Aw," Bailey said, "he's not, no, he's nothing, I mean, all Karl wants is somebody to go with him to the flicks." He yelled for Birdie.

She rushed in, carrying the phone and the Chinese slippers that Felice had given her. "I and Bailey," she explained to Red, "are going to see—"

"I told them."

"When did you make these plans?" Red asked, looking at his son, trying to get what was going on.

"Bailey called up—" Birdie started to say, quieted by the pressure of a hand on her head.

"Karl called a couple days ago," her cousin improvised smoothly, fixing Birdie with a glare that would dissolve ice cubes. "We'll probably be back late," he added, and then, at the door, in a sleight of hand that Red missed, he reached down and lifted the key from around Birdie's neck and dropped it on the counter.

"But how can we—?" She stopped. "Okay."

"See you later, Dad, Ella," Bailey said. "We gotta go."

I could not believe that boy. Calling Karl and asking him to come by, more than likely offering to pay for the theater tickets and a triple bucket of popcorn and maybe even a tank of gas. I hadn't thought Red and I would have a single moment alone.

"Good kid you got," I said, turning off the kitchen light.

"Your good influence," Red said, locking the back door.

We didn't need to get under the covers this time. We didn't even make it into the bedroom before I had my tongue in his mouth and his jeans all the way off. Before he'd pulled down my best love-making shorts and got his hands under my bra. I set my timer for two hours, figuring that was more than safe. And then we turned back the spread and threw ourselves on my clean navy sheets and tried all those ways you do to get inside somebody you love and let him get inside you, because you're one person and he's another, and it's always going to be that way, you being two people. Trying just for a little while to entangle, commingle, entwine enough to feel like one.

33

Later that week, I penned a letter to my mother. And whether I meant it that way, or it just happened, for the first time, every word I wrote was true.

Dear Mother,

Rufus and I took Birdie and Bailey to the old Episcopal church here, not far from our house. It was built stone by stone as an exact copy of St. Bartolph's in Cambridge, complete with flying buttresses, Gothic-arched windows, a wild little hollyhock-lined garden with daisies and pinks and bachelor buttons. And weathered tombstones on the side which appear older than the state of Louisiana.

I wore the button-front black linen dress you saw on a less happy occasion, and thought of how you and Terrell and I used to go on Sunday mornings together.

Rufus tells me that the roses from my very favorite catalogue, The Antique Rose Emporium, *are grown quite near to Austin, in the little town of Brenham, which is also the home of Blue Bell Supreme ice cream. And I plan to visit their wondrous gardens when next I come to see you.*

Daddy called to say that you had not changed your mind about attending the Agatha Adams Day celebration in Angelina County, and I am sorry for that. But Birdie and I, and our friends Felice and Mayfair Roberdeau, will be there in your name. In addition, a very dear friend of Terrell's has donated a baby grand piano in her memory to be given to the school where your former student is the principal. Please think of the children playing it every day.

I'm so glad you are still doing well and that Daddy has begun to walk in the house. Rufus has promised to check on you often for me.

                Love,

                Ella

ONE VIOLET LANE
OLD METAIRIE

A Note About the Author

Shelby Hearon was born in 1931 in Marion, Kentucky, lived for many years in Texas and New York, and now makes her home in Burlington, Vermont. She is the author of fifteen novels, including Footprints, Life Estates, *and* Owning Jolene, *which won an American Academy of Arts and Letters Literature Award. She has received an Ingram Merrill grant as well as fellowships for fiction from the John Simon Guggenheim Foundation and the National Endowment for the Arts, and she has twice won the Texas Institute of Letters fiction award. Married to physiologist William Halpern, she is the mother of a grown daughter and son.*

A Note on the Type

The text of this book was set in a typeface named Perpetua, designed by the British artist Eric Gill (1882–1940) and cut by the Monotype Corporation of London in 1928–30. Perpetua is a contemporary letter of original design, without any direct historical antecedents. The shapes of the roman letters basically derive from stonecutting, a form of lettering in which Gill was eminent. The italic is essentially an inclined roman. The general effect of the typeface in reading sizes is one of lightness and grace. The larger display sizes of the type are extremely elegant and form what is probably the most distinguished series of inscriptional letters cut in the present century.

Composed by Dix Type, Syracuse, New York
Printed and bound by R. R. Donnelley & Sons, Harrisonburg, Virginia
Designed by Iris Weinstein